SILKE'S RIDE

by

KEN FARMER

Cover Art by:
Ken Farmer
Adriana Girolami

AUTHOR

Ken Farmer didn't write his first full novel until he was sixty-nine years of age. He often wonders what the hell took him so long. At age seventy-eight...he's currently working on novel number thirty-four.

Ken spent thirty years raising cattle and quarter horses in Texas and forty-five years as a professional actor (after a stint in the Marine Corps). Those years gave him a background for storytelling...or as he has been known to say, "I've always been a bit of a bull---t artist, so writing novels kind of came naturally once it occurred to me I could put my stories down on paper."

Ken's writing style has been likened to a combination of Louis L'Amour and Terry C. Johnston with an occasional Hitchcockian twist...now that's a combination.

In addition to his love for writing fiction, he likes to teach acting, voice-over and writing workshops. His favorite expression is: "Just tell the damn story."

Writing has become Ken's second life: he has been a Marine, played collegiate football, been a Texas wildcatter, cattle and horse rancher, professional film and TV actor and director, and now...a novelist. Who knew?

Ken Farmer's dialogue flows like a beautiful western river...it's the gold standard...Carole Beers

ISBN-13: 978-1-7341765-3-7

Timber Creek Press
Imprint of Timber Creek Productions, LLC
312 N. Commerce St.
Gainesville, Texas 76240

Published by: Timber Creek Press
timbercreekpresss@yahoo.com
www.timbercreekpress.net
Twitter: @pagact
Facebook Book Page:
www.facebook.com/TimberCreekPress
Ken's email: pagact@yahoo.com
214-533-4964
© Copyright 2020 by Timber Creek Press. All rights reserved.

DEDICATION

This tome is dedicated to all my wonderful fans throughout the world. Without them, neither I nor any other author would be viable. I hope this third novel in the Silke Justice saga meets with your approval.

ACKNOWLEDGMENT

The author gratefully acknowledges Lt. Colonel Clyde DeLoach, USMC (Ret.), Buck Stienke, Terry Heflin - retired English Professor at Tarrant County College, award-winning, best-selling novelist Mary Deal, and Penny (Mom) Tucker for their invaluable help in proofing, beta reading and editing this novel.

This book is licensed for your personal enjoyment only. If you're reading this book and did not purchase it, or did not win it in an author/publisher contest, then please purchase your own copy. Thank you for respecting the hard work of the author.

This book, or parts thereof, may not be reproduced in any form with out prior written permission from the author.

This novel is a work of fiction…except the parts that aren't. Names, characters, places, and incidents are either the products of the author's imagination or are used fictitiously. Any resemblance to actual persons, living or dead, business establishments, events, or locales is entirely coincidental, except where they aren't.

TIMBER CREEK PRESS

CHAPTER ONE

BOBCAT CANYON
NEW MEXICO

"You saddle scum get your randy arses off my land…Not inclined to say it twice." Luz McPherson levered a round into her '73 Winchester and pointed it from her hip to the center of Ben Wilford's chest. "I'd soon as ventilate you as not."

"Now, Miz Mcpherson, ain't no need in…"

The wiry sixty-five year old western woman raised the rifle to her shoulder and moved her aim to his forehead. "One…"

Wilford's face blanched before it turned into a snarl. "You ain't heard the last of us, woman." He twisted in his saddle to the other three men to his right. "Let's git outta here…" He looked back at her. "Mark what I said."

"No, you mark what I say…Next time you won't be ridin' out of here…or anywhere else, for that matter."

Wilford glared at the gray-haired woman a moment, then viciously spurred his horse and rolled away from her porch.

Luz watched the four men gallop out of her front yard and head toward the front gate.

"I'm a-thinkin' we've just stirred a hornet's nest, Ma'am." The long, lanky, ranch foreman, Jake Tarbutton, pulled his Bull Durham makings from a vest pocket and built himself a quirly.

"I know, Jake…I know. Worked too hard buildin' this place an' that horse herd to let some

Johnny-come-lately, ne'er-do-well, come in here an' try to bully me off my land..." She shook her head. "Don't quite understand why they want my little two sections. Got more'n they can run cattle on now."

"Yessum, know what yer sayin'...but the thing is, they's jest the three of us an' Wilford's got least ten men workin' his place...mind three er four 'er gunhawks."

He stuck the roll-your-own in the corner of his mouth and popped his thumbnail on the head of a lucifer. The strike-anywhere match hissed and burst into a yellow flame as he held it to the twisted end.

Jake inhaled and blew a cloud of white smoke over his head. "We'll stand by you, Ma'am...you know that...It's jest..."

She lowered the hammer on her Winchester, turned and opened the screen door behind her. "Come inside with me a moment, Jake, got somethin' I want you to do." She leaned her rifle against the wall just inside the door.

"Yessum."

He flicked his half-smoked cigarette off the porch into the front yard with his middle finger and followed her inside the cool darkness.

They walked through the spacious, well-appointed, thick-walled, adobe ranch house to her office. The sweet scent of cinnamon *sopapillas* the ranch cook, Martina, had made for breakfast still lingered in the air.

Luz pulled out the chair at her large roll-top desk, took out a sheet of vellum and her pen. She dipped the point in her inkwell and wrote a short letter.

Luz coughed several times, blew on the ink a moment, folded the page, and handed it to Jake.

"Go into Santa Fe an' send this in a telegram to the name on the inside." She gave him a five dollar gold piece. "Don't stop nowhere...then git your butt back out here...Understand?"

"Yessum, be back 'bout mid-afternoon."

Jake spun on his heel and headed out the door.

Luz turned in her sheriff-style swivel chair and stared out the multi-paned window at Thompson Peak to the northeast in the Sangre de Cristo Mountains.

GAINESVILLE, TEXAS
SKEANS BOARDING HOUSE

The three story red brick Victorian home, converted to a boarding house, was located in the upscale area of cattle baron homes in south Gainesville on Dixon Street—known locally as 'Silk Panty Row'.

Pinkerton Detective, Silke Justice, Texas Ranger Riley Boston, Bone, and Loraine, and Padrino sat around the spacious parlor drinking after dinner coffee. It was just cool enough of a spring day outside for a fire in the brick fireplace.

Silke's almost grown black, blue-eyed half-wolf, Bear Dog, lay stretched out in front of the hearth.

Ranger Bodie Hickman's and his wife, Annabel's twins, five-year old Bass and Cassie Ann, were playing in the floor with nine year old Elizabeth Haas. She was the orphaned niece of Timothy and James McPherson who were killed in the battle with the inbred cannibal moonshiner clan over at Caddo Lake.

The dark-blonde proprietress, Faye Skeans, came through the wide doorway from the kitchen and through the dining room. She carried a large coffee pot.

"Anyone need a refill?"

"Thought you'd never ask, Faye." Bone held out his cup.

Loraine kicked the side of his leg. "Damn you, Bone, you could have gotten off your big butt and gotten it yourself, you wanted some."

Bone's enigmatic grin spread across his face. "Didn't know I wanted some more till Faye walked in here, Babe…Her coffee is the best."

Loraine gave him the stink eye. "Oh?…I'll remember that, mister."

"Uh-oh…Messed up, didn't I?"

Silke giggled. "You think?"

Faye grinned and filled Bone's cup. "Who else?"

Padrino held his out. "Believe I'll have a little freshen up, sweet Faye…I can say you make the best coffee in the world and not worry about it."

She gave him a special smile. "You would if you didn't."

He smiled back. "Good point, my dear."

Bear Dog shot to his feet, the hair along his back stood up and a deep growl rumbled from his throat as he stared at the foyer.

A moment later, a knock sounded at the front door.

"I'll get it, Faye, you have your hands full." Ranger Riley Boston got to his feet, set his cup on the mantle, and strode to the front door out in the foyer.

"Yes, miss, come right on in…My goodness you could pass for Silke's twin."

Silke jumped up from the dark green velvet settee when she heard Riley's statement. "Haven!"

Boston and a slightly younger duplicate of Silke Justice, except instead of strawberry-blonde, she had long sable hair with brown highlights, entered the parlor with the ranger. They also had the same striking cerulean blue eyes.

She and Silke embraced.

"Hey, cuz, what are you doing here?…" Silke stepped back. "My manners…Ya'll, this is my first cousin, Haven Justice. My Uncle Guss an' Aunt Janie's eldest, she's nineteen…Haven, the gentleman who escorted you in is Texas Ranger Riley Boston."

He nodded and smiled. "Miss."

She pointed. "That's Loraine and Darrell Bone…just call him, Bone. The gentleman next to the fire is Jethro Bartholomew Pereira, better known as Padrino, and the attractive lady with the coffee pot is our landlady, Faye Skeans."

Haven nodded at everyone and smiled. "How do you do, I certainly hope I'm not interruptin'." She glanced at the children on the floor and squatted down. "And who are these lovely children?"

Silke introduced the kids, "Bass and Cassie's mother and father, Annabel and Ranger Bodie Hickman are watchin' a play down to the theatre…they'll be home soon and I'm takin' care of Lizbeth here…tell you all about that later."

"It's all right, Silke…" Elizabeth looked at Haven. "My momma an' daddy an' both my uncles were killed by bad people…I don't really have anybody…but Silke." Her lower lip quivered slightly.

Haven embraced the thin, blonde, blue-eyed child. "I'm Silke's cousin…You got me too, now."

Elizabeth looked at Haven, and then up at Silke. "Ya'll could be sisters…'cept her hair is almost black." She felt of Haven's dark tresses.

Silke nodded. "So we've heard."

Bear Dog looked at Silke, then at Haven, cocked his head a moment, repeated the procedure, before he slunk toward Haven on his belly, rolled over to his back at her feet.

"Well, who are you?" She scratched his stomach.

"That's Bear Dog…an' you've apparently passed the test." Silke smiled.

"Or he thinks he's seein' double." Bone chuckled.

Loraine nodded. "That too."

Silke glanced at the carpet bag Haven had set down when she entered the room. "You're in your ridin' clothes…Are you goin' somewhere, Haven?"

She blushed and looked at her dusty boots with her jeans tucked in the top. "I…uh…was comin' here…to see you." The dark-haired beauty paused a second. "I want to be a Pinkerton, too."

Silke's eyebrows went up.

"Your horse out at the curb?" Padrino got to his feet.

"Yes, sir. He's tied to the hitching post."

Padrino grinned. "Sir was my daddy. Come on Riley let's go put it up back in the carriage house…'Spect it'll need currying and graining too."

"Yes, si…uh, Padrino. We left the house this mornin'…Haven't stopped for wood, water, nor coal."

Riley and Padrino headed out the front door. Ranger Boston turned his head before they left the room. "Got a name?"

She nodded. "*d'Artagnan*…I love Alexandre Dumas' work."

"Figures," muttered Padrino as they walked on out.

"How's my baby brother, Billy, Haven?"

"Oh, goodness, Silke, he's growin' like a weed. Asks about you all the time."

"Gotta get over to see him…Been so busy since momma an' daddy…well, since. We just got back from handlin' a case for the KATY railroad over to Caddo Lake."

Once more, Bear Dog growled toward the foyer.

Another knock sounded at the door.

Bone got to his feet. "I got it, Faye."

Again, they could hear voices out in the foyer.

"Brandi, what are you doin' here?…Come on in, girl."

Bone and Brandi Peterson from the Painted Lady Saloon came into the parlor.

"Brandi, is something the matter?" Loraine got to her feet and approached the tall dark-haired waitress.

"Yes, ma'am…Sort of. Got this telegram for Mister McPherson this afternoon an' Rube suggested I best bring it over to ya'll since you're takin' care of his niece an' all." She handed Silke the yellow envelope.

"Everythin' goin' all right over at the Lady, Brandi," asked Loraine.

"Yes, ma'am, business is good. That lawyer you sent to get the paperwork all fixed up doesn't know his back side from a gin whistle about a saloon, though…Pardon my language."

Silke opened the envelope, took the flimsy out, unfolded, and read it with Loraine looking over her shoulder.

Loraine's brow furrowed as Silke handed the missive to Bone. "Oh, my."

Silke looked down at the nine year old girl. "Did you know you have a grandmother, Lizbeth?"

"Yes, ma'am, I never met her…She moved to New Mexico from where they lived in New York 'fore I was born on account my mama said she was terrible sick an' couldn't breathe good…Unka Mack was goin' to take me to see her."

Bone raised both eyebrows as he read the telegram. "Lord love a duck."

Silke shook her head and took a breath. "Seems she doesn't know what happened to your mama and daddy and your uncles…She's got some troubles and was askin' Timothy and James for their help."

Elizabeth grabbed hold of Silke's arm and looked up—her eyes pleading. "We have to go…We gotta help my grandma."

Silke and Loraine exchanged glances…

§§§

CHAPTER TWO

CIRCLE W RANCH
NEW MEXICO

"Eb, you an' Pak slip over to the east line 'tween me an' that witch. Run a couple of her mares cross the creek and kill 'em."

Eb looked confused. "Won't she sic the sheriff on us?"

"Shore she will, mush for brains. Why do you think I said to run 'em cross the creek?"

Eb paused and furrowed his brow, then his eyes brightened. "Oh, I get it, they'll be on the Circle W, then…We jest tell the sheriff they was tresspassin'."

Wilford pitched what was left of his coffee into the weed-choked flower bed beside the porch and shook his head. "Your intelligence never ceases to amaze me Marsh."

"Well, hey, thankee, Boss, thankee kindly." A big grin spread across the weathered face of the wrangler.

"Take Ty with ya'll too. Have him keep watch for any of her hands while you an' Pak take care of bizness."

"Oh, shore, that's a good idee, Ern."

The Circle W foreman, Ernie Bryce, glanced at Wilford and got his confirming nod.

Eb and Pak walked down the four steps to the ground and out to their horses tied to the hitching rail in front.

Ty Needham, one of the ranch gunmen, leaning back against the rail, pitched his smoke to the ground, rubbed it out with the toe of his boot and walked around to the other side. He untied his blood bay gelding, stabbed a foot in the stirrup and swung his cadaverous form into the saddle.

"Anytime, ladies." His icy stare followed the two cowboys as they untied their horses.

Eb and Pak shot glances of dislike tinged with fear at the hatchet-faced gunhawk as they also mounted.

The foreman watched the three men ride out of the yard to the east.

"I still don't understand what you want that property for, Boss. We're under stocked as it is, plus got plenty water…an' she's got that big ridge runnin' through her place."

Wilford's dark brown eyes snapped over to his foreman. "Don't remember askin' for yer opinion, Bryce. Suggest you keep 'em to yerself."

GAINESVILLE, TEXAS
SKEANS BOARDING HOUSE

Riley and Padrino came back in the house through the kitchen because the large carriage house an paddock, where the horses were kept, was out back.

"*d'Artagnan's* a nice red roan…Good manners."

Haven nodded. "He takes care of me."

Riley rubbed both arms. "Temperature's droppin' some. Must be a late front comin' through."

He grabbed another piece of split oak from the wood box and laid it on the fire, turned his back to it and held his hands behind him.

Padrino was a seventy year old retired USMC Master Gunnery Sergeant who time-traveled to 1898 from 2018 through the same ancient Amerindian portal that Bone and Loraine came through. He sat back down in the oxblood leather Queen Anne wingback chair to the right of the hearth and picked up the day's copy of the *Gainesville Daily Register* he'd been reading before Silke's cousin came in.

"Do you need another cup of coffee, dear Jethro?"

He looked up at Faye and shook his head. "I'm fine, sweet Faye, but thanks for asking."

She turned to Haven. "Have you eaten, honey?"

She smiled, showing her dazzling white, even teeth. "I had some jerky on the ride over here, Ma'am."

"Oh, fiddlesticks, child, that's no kind of meal. I'll go fix you a nice thick sandwich from the pot roast we had from supper."

Haven looked at her boots. "That's all right, Ma'am, really…"

"I won't hear it…and quit callin' me, Ma'am…I surmise you'll be stayin' here with Silke, so you can call me Faye." She turned and headed toward the kitchen.

"You'll learn you can't argue with Faye, Haven." Silke had a big grin across her face. "Now, what's this about wantin' to be a Pink?" She patted the spot next to her on the dark green velvet love seat.

Haven sat down next to her cousin. "Well, you have to know that you've been my idol since I was a little girl…"

"I'm only four years older than you."

"I know, but I've always looked up to you an' I've been doin' a lot of studyin' about law enforcement…an' knew you joined the National

Pinkerton Detective Agency when you were twenty."

"But that was after the U.S. Marshal's Office turned me down."

"Know that, too, but this is what I want to do…Will you help me?" She looked at Silke with her big blue eyes.

Silke sighed. "I suppose so…but we'll have to see to your skills, first."

"Which ones?"

"Horsemanship, weapons, trackin', an' so on…What kind of gun do you have?"

"One just like yours…a .38-40 Peacemaker with ivory grips…It's in my bag."

"Well, how in the world…"

"I saw yours last time you were at the house an' I had Buck Stienke down to Lone Star Shooting Supply order it for me."

Silke looked askance at her. "Do you know how to use it?"

Haven blushed a little. "Been practicin' some…also got a '92 Winchester…same caliber."

"Well, that was smart."

"Suspect we'll be headin' out tomorrow for Santa Fe." Silke glanced at Elizabeth.

Bone set his empty cup back on his saucer on the Chippendale coffee table. "Count my bride and me in on that, Silke."

"And me," said Riley.

Silke glanced at the ranger. "Not likely, mister. You had a cracked skull an' its only been a week since you regained consciousness."

"Well, I'm goin' anyway."

Silke rose to her feet and put her fists on her shapely hips. "Now you listen to me, Riley Boston. I think that would be the dumbest thing you could do...You know I love you an' I'll not see you push your health that way. I'm kinda lookin' forward to havin' you around a while...We'll have to horseback from Amarillo to Santa Fe..."

Haven looked from Silke to Riley and back to Silke.

Padrino looked up from his paper. "Don't think so, Silke."

She turned to him. "Why's that?"

"You'll have to horseback, all right...but you'll have to do it from Childress."

"Childress?"

"That last high water on the Red damaged the trestle...Railroad is closed from Childress to

Amarillo till they get it fixed…Says here in the paper."

Loraine grinned. "Must be like in our time…if it's on the Internet, must be true."

"Do what? What's the internet?" Haven looked puzzled.

Silke looked at Loraine, and then at Bone. "She doesn't know."

Haven glanced to her cousin. "Know what?…What are ya'll talkin' about?"

Silke and Bone exchanged looks. Bone shrugged his massive shoulders and arched his eyebrows.

"Kind of a long story, Haven." Bone got to his feet and backed up to the fire.

She cocked her head. "Well?"

Twenty minutes later, Bone, Loraine, Padrino, and Silke finished telling Haven about how they came from one hundred and nineteen years in the future—plus about being cops in Gainesville in their time.

Elizabeth had a puzzled expression again and turned to Silke who just nodded.

"Explain more later, honey."

Haven looked around the parlor. "Ya'll are serious, aren't you?"

Bone smiled. "Hope to shout, little lady…Surprised us too, to start with."

Silke got to her feet, walked to the hat tree in the hall and removed her Smith & Wesson 500, .50 caliber pistol from its holster. She unloaded it, strode back over and handed it to Haven.

"Padrino brought me this from the future…Bone carries one just like it. Keep my .38-40 in my saddlebags as a backup."

Haven lifted it and looked at the cylinder. "My God, it's like a hand cannon…A .50 caliber?"

"Uh-huh. When you shoot somebody with it…they stay shot."

Bone nodded. "An' that's fact, girl."

"Loraine carries a .45 caliber semiautomatic…Can fire eight rounds as fast as you can pull the trigger."

Haven blinked several times. "My, my." Then she looked at Bone and Loraine. "Are ya'll goin' back?"

They exchanged glances again.

Loraine took a breath. "Haven't decided yet…Kinda like it here."

"Goes double for me." Padrino looked at Faye for a long moment.

She blushed. "I'm glad."

Silke turned to Riley again. "That's even a longer ride from Childress to Santa Fe…plus across Palo Duro Canyon an' the *Llano Estacado*."

"Yeah, but…"

"No buts, mister…Tell you what, sweetheart. If Doctor Wellman says it's all right, then you can go…Deal?"

Riley grimaced. "Deal…You already know, don't you?"

Silke smiled and nodded. "He told me when he let you out of the clinic that you weren't to go near a horse for at least a month…You could start that bleeding inside your head again…If it weren't for Bone, Loraine, and Lucy, you wouldn't be here now."

Haven looked puzzled again. "Lucy?"

Bone stepped back over from the fireplace and sat down heavily on the couch. "Here we go."

She looked at the big man. "What do you mean, 'here we go'?"

Another twenty minutes later, they had finished telling Haven about Lucy, whose real name was *Annuna*, being an *Anunnaki* from the planet Tyrin across the galaxy, and crashing her ship at Aurora, Texas on April 17, 1897.

Elizabeth still had a puzzled expression, but she didn't say anything.

Haven's goddess-like face turned slightly pale. "Read about the crash in the Dallas Morning News…Didn't know there was a survivor…Am I goin' to meet her, too?"

Silke nodded. "Most likely."

Haven shook her head. "Oh, Lord…what have I gotten myself into?"

§§§

CHAPTER THREE

SKEANS BOARDING HOUSE

Silke set her cup down, picked up her white linen napkin, blotted her mouth and pushed back from the breakfast table in the kitchen.

"Best run down to the bank and get some travelin' money, then go by Martin's for supplies."

She looked at Haven. "Wanta go, cuz?"

"Sure, I need some things, too."

Loraine stirred a spoonful of sugar in her coffee. "Need us to go, Silke?"

"Oh, don't think so, Loraine, unless ya'll need somethin' special."

Bone and Loraine exchanged glances.

"Think we're good, except for a side of bacon."

"Was goin' to get that anyway…plus some put-by beans, more Arbuckle's, an' pickled peaches to go with what we still have from the Caddo trip."

"Can I go, Silke?" Elizabeth looked up from her almost finished bowl of oatmeal.

"Why don't you stay here and pack your bag, honey…Are you goin' to take your grandma a present?"

"Uh-huh…" She reached into her dress pocket and pulled out one of her wine fresh water pearls—over a third inch in diameter. "Wanted her to have one of the nice ones my cousin Maggie left us…Wish I could put it on a necklace."

Silke held out her hand. "Let me have it, Lizbeth, Haven an' I'll go by Kinne's jewelry store on California Street…Bet they can put it on a nice gold chain…What do you think?"

The little girl clapped her hands together several times and squealed. "Oh, goody…Thank you."

"Wouldn't hurt to put the rest of those pearls in a safe deposit box at the bank, either."

"Good idea, Padrino." Silke turned back to Elizabeth. "Would you go upstairs and get the rest of the pearls, honey?"

Faye brought the coffee pot over to the table to fill Bone's cup. "What about havin' William Kinne down at Kinne's Jewelers evaluate them?…He possibly might want to buy some."

Silke glanced at Faye. "That's even better…Want me to do that, Lizbeth?"

She nodded. "If you think so…I'll run get 'em. May I be excused?"

"Of course, dear," responded Faye.

Elizabeth jumped down from her chair, ran into the hall, and up the stairs to the room she was sharing with the twins.

Bone looked up. "Be interesting to see what those pearls are worth…Some of them are quite sizable…with remarkable coloring."

"Amazing that Maggie was able to accumulate that many…Must be two and a half…maybe three pounds," added Loraine.

Bone nodded. "She said the Sasquatch had been eating the clams at that spot for years an' just throwing the pearls away along with the shattered shells."

Elizabeth came back in with the Arbuckle's can almost filled with the blue, white, rust, and wine colored pearls. "I kept some to remind me of Maggie."

Silke took the can from her and kissed her forehead. "That's real sweet, Lizbeth." She looked at Haven. "Shall we, cuz?"

"I'm with you."

"Let me get my gunbelt an' we'll go saddle up."

"Gonna wear your gun?"

"One thing you'll learn about bein' a Pinkerton, Haven, always go armed…just like if you were a Deputy Marshal or police officer."

Loraine nodded. "Absolutely…'better to have and not need than need and not have'."

Padrino had a slight smile. "Originally said by Franz Kafka, Bohemian novelist in *The Metamorphosis*."

"Knew I heard it somewhere," commented Bone. "We have a western novelist in our time by the name of Louis L'Amour who said in his novel, *The Daybreakers*, 'Violence is an evil thing, but when the guns are all in the hands of the men without respect for human rights, then men are really in trouble'."

Loraine shook her head. "Only my Bone."

FIRST STATE BANK

There were only two customers inside the bank, an elderly white-haired woman and an overweight middle-aged man with a cane. They were at two of the three teller windows.

Two young men with blue bandannas over the bottom half of their faces, entered the right side of the nine-foot tall double half-glass front doors.

Both were brandishing older type revolvers.

The leading man waved his pistol around. "Everybody down on the floor! This here's a hold..."

"Oh, shut up, Bobby Ray, they know what it is."

The two customers painfully laid down on the hardwood floor.

The first robber turned. "Bobby Ray? Why'd you call me…"

"I said shut up!"

The apparent leader was at one of the half-barred windows. He slid the teller an old flour sack across the counter. "Fill it up, just the paper money an' don't do nothin' stupid, hear?"

The teller took the sack. "Yes, sir…It'll take just a minute.

The robber looked at the teller's name plate on the counter. "Uh…James Wilkins…I, uh, know where you live."

Wilkins eyes went wide as he started stuffing all the cash from his drawer into the sack. "Yes, sir… Please don't hurt me…Got a wife an' two kids."

The second robber watching the door and the customers on the floor glanced at the one at the teller's window and stepped over to him. "Hurry up, Harlan!"

He grabbed the sack from Wilkins and spun around. "You idiot!"

"What?…What?"

"Never mind…Let's go."

Unbeknownst to the two desperadoes, Silke and Haven had come in the front door while the two were arguing over in front of the teller's windows.

Silke bumped Haven's hip with her hand and moved to her left, indicating for her cousin to move to the right.

Harlan turned to the other he called Bobby Ray. "Your bread just ain't real done, you know that?"

"Huh? What do you mean, Harlan?"

Harlan slapped Bobby Ray upside his head, knocking his hat to the floor.

He bent over to pick up the battered old fedora and noticed the two girls on either side of the door.

Silke flashed a grin at the two masked robbers. "He means you're dumber'n a bucket of rocks."

"Huh?"

Harlan spun around and pointed his pistol first at Silke, then at Haven, who was also grinning.

Silke continued, "Why don't you boys put those shooters down before someone gets hurt."

"Well, looks to me like we're holdin' the guns, lady…So, I'd say we're the ones givin' the orders 'round here." Harlan still couldn't decide who to point his pistol at.

"Oh, that doesn't mean much…You see…" Silke pointed with her left hand. "Ya'll haven't even cocked 'em."

Harlan and the one called Bobby Ray both looked down at their guns.

Silke drew the big Smith and Wesson .50 cal, cocking it as it came out of the holster.

Haven slicked her .38-40 out in a blinding blur at the same time, also cocking it as it cleared the leather.

The two would-be holdup men's eyes snapped up at the sound of the hammers locking into place.

Silke grinned again. "End of the trail, boys…Drop those shooters to the floor or suffer the consequences…Your choice."

The two sets of eyes above the bandannas got big as saucers.

The one called Bobby Ray looked at his brother. "What do we do, Harlan?"

Haven spoke up, "Wouldn't be askin' him, sunshine, I'm bettin' he's the one that got you into this mess…Now, like my cousin said…'Drop 'em'."

The two men dropped their rusty revolvers to the floor and raised their hands.

"Just who are ya'll anyways?" asked Harlan.

Silke shook her head. "If we told you that, we'd just have to go ahead an' kill you anyway…Let's say that this is your lucky day."

"Huh? What do you mean?"

"That you didn't die doin' somethin' stupid…Maybe it taught you a lesson." Silke looked at the first teller. "You want to run down an' get Marshal Farmer, so he can take these ne'er-do-wells off our hands…We got things to do an' places to go."

Wilkins came from around the counter and ran toward the door. "Yes, Ma'am, be right back."

"Use one of these idiot's horses. 'Spect they're out front there," suggested Haven.

Silke waved the hand cannon. "Now, you two, lay down on the floor, spread your arms and legs…and trust me, you don't want to move after you get down there."

"Yes, Ma'am," both said simultaneously as Silke stepped over and kicked their guns to the side, holstered her 500 and helped the elderly woman to her feet.

Haven assisted the overweight man up and handed him his cane.

"Thank you, Miss. Gittin' down ain't too much of a problem at my age, but the gittin' up is a whole 'nother story…Shore 'preciate you young ladies comin' in when you did."

She smiled. "Glad to help."

Silke looked at Haven as she helped the woman to her feet. "I caught you out of the corner of my eye, cuz…Never even saw you draw."

Haven blushed. "Told you I've been practicin'."

§§§

CHAPTER FOUR

FIRST STATE BANK

Town Marshal Kenneth Farmer limped through the front door being held open by the teller, James Wilkins. He was followed by his young deputy, Billy Webber.

Marshal Farmer pointed at the two would-be bank robbers with his bull penis cane. "Well, well,

Harlan an' Jeb Casey. What the devil have you boys done?"

Harlan glanced at Jeb then at Farmer. "Hydee, Marshal, we…uh…well, we's gonna go to the port down to Houston an' see 'bout work an'…Uh…didn't have no money to git there."

"Uh-huh…Not smart, but I'm not surprised." Farmer turned to his deputy. "Shackle 'em, Billy while they're on the floor, then get their guns…There's one there an' the other's over yonder by the counter."

"Yessir, Marshal." He shackled the two would-be robbers while they lay on their stomachs, stepped over and picked up their old Navy Colt converted revolvers. "Say, looky here, Marshal, neither of these 'er loaded."

The marshal shook his head and grinned. "Boys, you best count your lucky fairy godmother you're still breathin'." He looked at Silke and Haven. "Know both these girls an' they can shoot the flies off'n a bull's butt at thirty yards…Pardon my language, ladies." He tipped his hat. "Good thing you did what they told you…Ya'll musta been carryin' your brains in your back pockets."

Jeb glanced over at Harlan. "We got a fairy godmother?"

"Reckon we do now."

"Get 'em up an' take 'em out to the buckboard, Billy. Be out there in a minute."

"Yessir…Awright, you two. Let's go." He helped Harlan first, then Jeb to their feet and walked them out the front door.

The marshal turned to Silke and Haven. "Thanks, girls. Know you could have shot those two numb-nuts but glad you didn't…Not the sharpest knives in the drawer, but overall, not bad kids…Just got shorted on the good upbringin' part."

"What's goin' to happen to 'em, Marshal?"

He smiled. "Oh, Haven, probably keep 'em in my hoosegow a week or so, an' then make 'em work out a fine doin' community service…scoopin' up horse apples from the streets an' such…Give me a chance to work on 'em some…" His blue eyes twinkled. "…Know what I mean?"

They exchanged glances and nodded.

Marshal Farmer tipped his hat. "How's your folks, Haven?"

"They're doin' fine, Marshal."

He looked at Silke. "Sure awful 'bout your mama an' daddy, Silke...Understand you got 'em tracked down with Marshal Bass Reeves."

Silke nodded. "They paid the price."

He tipped his hat. "Ya'll have a nice day, hear?"

"You, too," they replied together and stepped over to one of the teller windows as the marshal exited the front doors.

The ornate wood counter and windows smelled of fresh lemon oil polish.

"James, need some cash from my account, please."

He nodded. "Yes, Miss Silke, how much you aneedin' today?"

"Oh, think a couple hundred in ten dollar bills and two double eagles should do it...We got a little trip to Santa Fe to make."

He counted out twenty tens on the counter, slid the stack under the window, and laid the two gold coins beside the paper money. "Anythin' for you, Miss Haven?"

"Probably fifty in fives an' ten in Morgan silver dollars for me."

He pushed out the fives and the silver coins along with two withdrawal slips for them to sign.

They signed the papers and handed them back.

"If you need any more, just wire the bank an' I'll take care of it for you."

It was obvious the young bank teller was smitten by the two very attractive ladies.

"Thank you, James, that is so sweet." Haven batted her cerulean blue eyes.

He ducked his head and blushed. "Thank you, Miss Haven…Be a pleasure."

They turned and made their way to the front door.

Silke glanced at her cousin. "You did that on purpose."

Haven grinned. "Uh-huh."

PAP CLARK'S LIVERY

"Need a good stout pack horse, Pap…Got one?"

The elderly, white-haired hostler removed his pipe from his mouth. "How far, how long, an' where ya'll headin', Bone?"

"Santa Fe...Gotta horseback from Childress. Bridge's out over the Red, so can't get to Amarillo."

"Gonna cross the Palo Duro and The Staked Plains, then, areyuh?"

Loraine nodded. "That's the plan."

"Recommend a mule then. Got more bottom than a horse, specially over parched or rough country...Got just the one...That big Tennessee black nose out in the corral...Name's Ted."

Bone, Loraine, and Bear Dog followed Pap over to the corral.

"Looks like a stout fella. Got good manners?" Bone looked the dark red mule over.

"Most of the time...Might take a nip outta your shoulder or backside if'n he thinks you're bein' mean to him, though...Won't tolerate it...Let you know what's what in short order."

Ted walked over to the fence and hung his big black nose over the top plank. Bear Dog raised up on his back legs and put his front paws on the second plank from the top so he and Ted could sniff each other.

Their noses touched for a moment—Ted's thick tongue lolled out and licked Bear Dog under his chin. The wolf dog returned the affection.

Pap spat to the side. "Well, would you looky there…Never seen him do that 'fore."

Loraine grinned. "That's Bear Dog…He's a quick judge of character. Guess he approves of Ted."

Bone nodded. "We'll take him…Got a couple of panniers?"

"Shore…Mount 'em for you. Ya'll kin settle up when you git back…Rental fee is three dollars a week. 'Spect him to look the same as he does now when ya'll git back." He took a draw from his pipe and blew out an aromatic cloud of blue smoke. "How many of ya'll're goin'?"

"Four, Pap…Oh, dang! Almost forgot. Need a mount for a nine year old girl, too."

The venerable long time hostler scratched the stubble on his chin for a short moment. "Got just the thing…Little tricolor paint mustang geldin' over in the back corral. Rides good an' is gentle. I'll git him ready too…Name's Calico."

Bone nodded. “Sounds good, Pap, we’ll be back in about an hour…Gotta catch the noon westbound.”

“I’ll load enough grain in the panniers for the six head…an’ water bags, too. You’ll need it acrossin’ the *Llano Estacado*. There’s some awful dry stretches.”

“So we’ve heard.” Bone turned to Loraine. “Ready, Pard?”

“Waitin’ on you.”

KINNE’S JEWELRY

Silke set the coffee canister on the glass counter and popped the lid off. The owner, William Kinne, took several of the pearls out and laid them on a swatch of black velvet cloth next to the can. He slipped on a pair of white cotton gloves, placed his loop in his right eye, picked up one of the blue pearls and held it up to the eyepiece, rolling it around between his thumb and forefinger.

“Oh, my, my, my…This is exquisite. Never seen such clarity.” He set the blue one down and got a large wine one. “My goodness gracious. I’ve never seen one quite this color either, and the luster is absolutely superlative." He looked up at Silke. "Where did you say these pearls came from?"

"Lake Caddo…on the Louisiana side."

"Did ya'll find these?"

Silke shook her head. "A young girl found them…uh, over a period of several years. Don't know exactly where, though. She…uh, passed away an' left these to a cousin of hers…I take care of her."

The bell at the front door tinkled as a man in a three piece suit entered.

"Goodness, goodness, goodness. It would take me some time to catalogue all these…but I can tell you now that I won't be able to afford to buy them all…Off the top of my head I'm goin' to say they're worth from three hundred up to two thousand dollars." He glanced at the new customer. "I'll be with you in a moment, sir."

"That's fine. Take your time." He leaned over and studied the gold pocket watches in the glass case.

"Oh, my…For the can?"

Kinne's kind hazel eyes looked at her and he had a wry grin on his face. "No, my dear…each."

Silke and Haven both brought their hands to their mouths and gasped.

"Oh, my Lord…I never…" Silke reached in her shirt pocket and brought out a piece of white cotton cloth from Faye's sewing room, unfolded it and laid it on the counter.

In the center of the swatch was the marble-sized, perfectly round, wine pearl Elizabeth gave her that morning.

"The little girl wants to give this one to her grandmother in Santa Fe, but she wanted it on a necklace…Can you do something like that?"

William picked up the large pearl and held it in the palm of his hand. "Oh, my…Yes, of course. Let me mount this in a gold setting with a gold chain…Won't take but a few moments."

He went back to his workbench and selected a filigreed mounting with a chain—set the pearl in the center and clamped the four small gold dogs against the side of the pearl, firmly holding it in place, and then polished it with his jeweler's cloth.

"Here you are. Let me put this in a velvet box, I'm afraid you'll have to wrap it yourself."

"Thank you." Silke held up the almost half-inch gleaming wine pearl hanging from the gold chain.

"Oh, my goodness," said Haven. "That is absolutely gorgeous. I'm sure Lizbeth's grandmother is going to love it."

Kinne selected five sample pearls of different sizes and colors, snapped the lid back on the square canister, and handed it to Silke…he put the pearls in a small velvet drawstring pouch and pulled the opening closed.

"I'll show these to my gems representative and get an idea from him as to value. I'll let you know…you can bring them back, then. I'd suggest you put these with the bank for safe keeping until I get with him…We can settle up then."

"Good idea, we'll be gone a few weeks to New Mexico an' will come in when we get back."

"That will be fine. Look forward to seeing you again. Where are you staying when you're in town?"

"At Faye Skeans…"

"Of course, know Faye well. I'll contact you there."

"Bye-bye, now," said Silke as she and Haven left through the front door, tinkling the bell attached to the header again.

Kinne turned to the male customer. "Yes, sir, how may I help you today?"

The man watched the door close behind Silke and Haven—then looked at the jeweler…

§§§

CHAPTER FIVE

BAR M RANCH
NEW MEXICO

Jake Tarbutton knocked on the doorjam of Luz's office.

"Come on in, Jake, I'm just workin' on the ledgers."

The lanky foreman of the Bar M tentatively walked inside. He held his sweat-stained gray felt hat in both hands, twisting and turning it as he approached Luz at her roll top desk.

"Miz McPherson…"

She turned in her chair to face him. "What is it?"

"Uh…we lost two mares, Ma'am…I'm terrible sorry."

"What do you mean, 'lost two'?"

"Well…uh, couple of the boys found 'em over to Hard Bottom Creek…Dead, Ma'am."

"Dead?"

"Yessum."

"How?"

"Uh…they wuz shot, Ma'am."

Luz jumped to her feet. "What? What are you sayin'?…Which ones were they?"

"It wuz, Belle an' Daisy, Ma'am. You know how they always hung together."

"Who done it?"

"The boys figure it was Wilford's hands."

"That son-of-a…Send somebody for Sheriff Russell…Time we stopped this."

"'Fraid won't do no good, Ma'am."

"Why's that?"

"They was on the 'tuther side of the creek…on Circle W land."

"Our horses don't cross that creek. Got plenty graze on this side…an' the water's most always over belly deep." Luz paused in thought for a moment, nodded, and set her jaw. "That bastard had his men drive 'em across just so they could shoot 'em for bein' on his land…That evil offspring of *Erebus*…" She turned and stared out the window for a moment.

Luz turned back around and looked up at Jake as tears slowly rolled down her cheeks. "How far along were they?"

"Belle was a good six months an' Daisy weren't too far behind."

KINNE'S JEWELRY

William Kinne walked up to the man in the three piece suit on the other side of the counter after Silke and Haven had left. "Yessir, now, how may I help you today, sir?"

"Were those pearls those girls had in that can?"

"They were indeed, sir…fresh water pearls. I've never seen such color and luster."

"An' that Arbuckle's cannister was full?"

Kinne nodded. "It was."

"My, my, my."

He looked out the door as Silke glanced up at the large clock atop a painted black cast-iron pole in front of the store, said something to Haven and put the canister in her saddle bags.

They untied their mounts from the metal ring posts, swung lithely into the saddles, and rode toward the east at a smooth single-foot trot.

"Noticed you lookin' at the pocket watches. Are you interested in acquiring one, sir?"

He looked back at the jeweler. "Uh…didn't see anything that struck my fancy. Was just browsing anyway." He touched his gray Homberg hat. "Much obliged."

"Come back and see us."

He stepped toward the door, walked outside and looked down the red-bricked street.

Kinne watched him mount his blood bay gelding and ride off in the same direction Silke and Haven had taken.

CALIFORNIA STREET

"We gonna stop at the bank like Mister Kinne said?"

Silke shook her head. "No time, Haven."

"What I figured when you looked at that clock outside his shop."

"Got to stop at Martins for our supplies, an' then finish our packin', so we can make the train…Have to get the horses loaded down to the yard…an' that takes a little time."

They reined over to Martin's Mercantile, dismounted, tied up, and went inside.

The man on the blood bay pulled up under a large red oak a block back of Silke and Haven and watched them go inside the store.

He sat his horse for a moment before he trotted off toward the Katy Depot.

Twenty minutes later, Silke and Haven stepped out of Martin's. They carried two tow sacks of supplies each which they tied together and slung over behind their cantles.

The girls mounted up and trotted on down another block to Dixon Street, turned south and continued the three blocks to the boarding house.

SKEANS BOARDING HOUSE

They reined up next to three horses and a mule tied up in front at the edge of the street—Bone's black seventeen hand gelding, Hildebrandt, Loraine's bright red sorrel mare, Sweet Face, the paint pony, Calico, and Ted, the big dark red Tennessee black-nosed pack mule.

Bone and Loraine came down the steps from the wide, wrap-around front porch and walked out to the girls as they stepped down.

Bear Dog was right on their heels. He raised up on his back legs and walked toward Silke so he could lean his head against her shapely hip. She laid her hand on his broad head and scratched behind his ears. His blue eyes closed in pleasure at the attention of his mistress.

"Took ya'll long enough. We need to cut a chodie packing this stuff up in the panniers and get down to the depot."

Bone pulled the sacks off of Silke's lineback dun, *Lakná*, while Loraine grabbed the ones from Haven's red roan, *d'Artagnan*.

He and Loraine started packing the goods in the panniers with the items they had already loaded from the house.

"We had to interrupt a couple of dimwits tryin' to hold up the bank an' then wait for Marshal Farmer to come down an' haul 'em off to his jail."

Loraine looked over at Silke. "Any shootin'?"

Silke giggled. "Their guns weren't even loaded…Sure glad they dropped 'em when Haven an' I told 'em to…"

"We came close to pluggin' 'em anyway when they pointed 'em at us," interrupted Haven.

Bone shook his head. "I probably would have. Part of our cop training in our time…Bad guy points a gun at you…he's a dead man. No warning, no discussion…You just don't know if or when they might pull the trigger."

"I could tell they didn't want to shoot anybody. Just a couple of scared kids trying to bluff their way into gettin' some money."

Loraine nodded. "Like Bone said, though, in our time it would have just gotten them dead."

"You're probably right, Loraine…I could have been wrong." Silke glanced at Haven. "Know better next time, right, cuz?"

Bone grinned. "There won't always be a next time, Silke…Count it as a lesson learned."

"True. Let's go get our bags, Haven…Plus Lizbeth'll want to see this pearl we had mounted for her grandmother."

The two near twin cousins strode up the flagstone walk to the steps, then on the porch, and inside.

Elizabeth met them as they entered the foyer. "You're back, you're back…Got my bag packed an' I'm ready." She beamed.

Silke knelt down and hugged the nine year old. "That's wonderful, honey. Got somethin' to show you." She reached in her jacket pocket and brought out the small rectangular velvet box and handed it to her.

Elizabeth opened it to see the wine pearl in the gold setting in the center of the box with the gold chain spread from side to side on a soft white satin bed.

She gasped—her eyes filled with tears. "Oh, this is so beautiful." Elizabeth looked up at Silke as the first tear rolled from her big blue eyes. "Thank you, thank you…I can't wait to give this to my grandma." She closed the box and hugged Silke.

Haven's eyes also filled with tears as she watched. "Your grandmother'll love it, Lizbeth." She placed her hand on the child's shoulder.

The little girl looked over at the sable-haired beauty and nodded as more tears flowed down her cheeks.

Faye entered the foyer with a brown paper sack, folded at the top. "I made ya'll some sandwiches for the train ride. There's also some of my special carrot cake in here, too." She handed the sack to Haven.

Ranger Riley Boston followed right behind her.

"Thank you, so much, Faye, I know we'll enjoy them…an' the cake." She hugged her neck.

Bone and Loraine came in the front door.

"All right, ladies, get your bags, we best scoot."

He picked up Elizabeth's carpet bag that was sitting beside her foot.

"Now, ya'll be careful, hear?" Faye hugged each one. "Send me a telegram when you get there." Her brown eyes twinkled. "May have a surprise when you get back." She glanced at

Padrino as he came through the door from the kitchen.

“Do we get a guess?” Bone looked at her, then at his godfather.

“No.” Padrino shook his head. “Wouldn’t be a surprise, then.”

The big man grinned. “Right.”

Silke and Riley embraced and kissed.

“I’ll miss you.”

“Miss you, too, Ranger. You follow Doc Wellman’s instructions…Hear?”

“I will. Ya’ll keep an eye out goin’ through the Palo Duro and the Staked Plains…Hear tell there’s still some renegade Injuns an’ outlaws hangin’ out ‘round there.”

“We will.” She kissed him again.

They all headed out the door and down the walk to their mounts.

Bone picked Elizabeth up and set her in the saddle of the paint. “This is my pony, his name’s Calico…he’s nice.”

Silke stepped up into *Lakná’s* saddle “He certainly is. Got a good shoulder slope on him, bet he’s smooth.”

Loraine nodded. "Pap Clark said he was…and real gentle too."

They all waved good bye as they headed north on Dixon Street toward the depot.

Almost ten minutes later, they reined into the stock corral area next to the tracks. The railroad hostler walked up with his colored helper.

"Howdy, folks, name's Slim, this here's Otho, he's my right arm…Catchin' the train, airye?"

Bone nodded. "That we are my friend. To the end of the line at Childress…today. Hope they'll have the bridge repaired over the Red by the time we head back this way."

"Said they'd have it all put back together in 'bout ten days…give er take. Mostly give, I 'spect."

"Figured…Need any help loadin' and untacking the stock?"

Slim chuckled. "Been doin' this since bully was a pup, sonny…Won't take me an' Otho long. Ya'll go 'head an' git settled…Room in car number three yonder." He pointed.

Bone nodded. "Much obliged."

They headed toward the passenger car he referenced. Silke clipped a leash on Bear Dog's leather collar, so the other passengers wouldn't be concerned about the big black wolf dog.

Bone assisted Elizabeth and the ladies up the metal stairway to the car. He followed behind them. They carried their carpet bags, saddlebags and long guns

Loraine pointed at a large open space in the overhead shelf on the right side. "There's room here, ya'll."

Bone took the bag and rifle from his 5'3" wife and placed her gear along with his in the rack.

Silke and Haven, both at 5'8", were able to stow their own guns and bags.

Bone and Loraine took seats on the right side of the car halfway to the front while Silke, Haven, Elizabeth, and Bear Dog sat just across the aisle in facing seats.

The girls failed to pay any attention to the man in a three piece tweed suit and gray Hamburg hat sitting just behind them…

§§§

CHAPTER SIX

NORTH TEXAS

The big black 4x4x2 locomotive chugged along the bucolic countryside to the west paralleling the Red River a few miles to the north. A plume of black coal smoke boiled from her short stack.

Elizabeth had her pug nose pressed to the window and watched the rolling grasslands pass by on the south side of the tracks. “Oh, it’s so beautiful…Look how the tops of the grass moves like waves on water.”

“Had you never been away from Denison, before, Lizbeth?”

The nine year old turned to Silke and shook her head. “Uh-uh…Least not that I remember. We moved there when I was still little so daddy could work for the railroad…All I saw when Unka Mack an’ me went to Lake Caddo an’ Unka James’ house was lotsa trees an’ that black spooky lake.”

“Well, you’ll be seeing a lot of different country between here and Santa Fe.”

The man in the tweed suit sitting behind them tapped Silke on her shoulder. “Beg your pardon, Miss, didn’t mean to eavesdrop, but did I hear you say ya’ll were traveling to Santa Fe?”

Silke turned in the seat to look over her shoulder. “Yes, we are. We’re taking Lizbeth here to see her grandmother.”

“How do you do, young lady?”

“I do fine, thank you, sir.”

He nodded and smiled at Elizabeth before he turned back to Silke. “That’s very nice…I take it you’re horsebacking from Childress, then?”

"Apparently we don't have a choice since the bridge across the Red is under repair."

"Yes, very true. I'm going to Santa Fe myself…on a business trip. Possibly we could travel together?"

Silke smiled at the handsome, well-dressed businessman and nodded at Bone sitting across the aisleway with Loraine. "I suggest you confer with Deputy Bone, there. He an' his wife are travelin' with us."

"Deputy?"

She nodded. "They're both deputy sheriffs and part-time Deputy US Marshals back in Cooke County.

He turned in his seat to look at the big man and Loraine. "Yes, I'll do that when we reach Childress or maybe when we stop for water…By the way, my name is Reginald Berkley, folks just call me Reg."

"What kind of business are you in, Mister Berkley?"

"Reg, please…I'm uh…in land acquisitions and mining."

"Reg…I'm Silke Justice." She nodded at the seat across from her. "That's my cousin Haven Justice, and this is my charge, Elizabeth Haas."

He removed his hat. "It's a pleasure, Miss Justice."

She smiled. "You may call me Silke."

His eyebrows went up. "Silke? That's Latin for Heavenly isn't it?"

"Very good, Reg, not many know that."

"My mother made sure I studied Latin, the Letters, and the classics in school."

"Oh, really, how interestin'...My mother was a school teacher...taught Latin and History and just loved the name Silke...sometimes referred to as Celia."

He smiled, showing his even white teeth. "Yes, indeed and your cousin, Haven's name, meaning safety or refuge, was derived from Eden or Zion, for that matter."

Silke looked at her cousin. "Did you hear that, Haven?"

She nodded. "Mama said she asked your mother for suggestions when I was born an' that's where Haven came from."

Reg nodded. "Fascinating." He glanced back to Silke. "Your mother and father must be special people."

She glanced out the window at the passing countryside, then back. "Yes…they were."

"Were?"

Silke bit her lower lip. "They were murdered a few months back by a gang of outlaws."

"Oh, I'm so sorry, how terrible for you. I hope they were brought to justice…to coin a phrase."

She pursed her lips tightly. "Yes, they were…Each an' every one of them." Her cerulean eyes flashed.

"Oh, my…I take it you were involved in the hunt?"

Silke's jaw was set. "I was." She looked back out the window. "Along with the Bones an' Deputy US Marshal Bass Reeves."

"Bass Reeves?…Goodness, heard of him. One of the best…I'm told."

"He is that…I learned a lot from him."

"Are you in law enforcement also?"

"Sort of…I'm an agent with the Pinkerton National Detective Agency."

"You're a detective?"

"For over two years, now…I'm trainin' Haven to be one, too."

"I certainly hope we can work out something when we reach Childress...I would feel much safer traveling with the likes of your group."

CIRCLE W RANCH
NEW MEXICO

Ben Wilford walked out to the round pole corral where several of his hands were busting some broncs. He propped a booted foot on the bottom rail and his elbows on the top one.

"Ernie, git over here."

The ranch foreman, Ernie Bryce, sauntered over to the fence from the center snubbing post where they had a fresh mustang tied up short with a tow sack wrapped around his eyes.

"What's up, Boss?"

"Time for the next step on Miz McPherson."

"Right. Whatcha got in mind?"

"Take a couple of the boys, cut out some of our best mares an' drive 'em onto her property. Make sure they got our brand on 'em an' mix 'em in with her herd."

"Our best stock?"

Wilford spat a stream of viscous brown tobacco juice to the side that kicked up a small plume of dust when it hit the dry ground. "Uh-huh…If you wuz gonna steal some horses…wouldn't you want the best?"

Ernie frowned, slightly confused. "Uh…yeah, reckon I…" His brown eyes brightened. "Oh!" He grinned and nodded. "Right."

WICHITA FALLS, TEXAS

The train slowed as it pulled into the depot, blowing huge clouds of steam from her relief valves.

Inside, a blue-clad conductor strolled through the passenger cars. "Wichita Falls…water stop. Get out an' stretch if you like. We will leave in fifteen minutes."

He repeated the message in each of the three passenger cars.

Silke got to her feet. "Come on Bear Dog, let's go take a walk. Want to?"

The big black wolf-dog *woo-wooed* at her and bounced on his front paws in anticipation. He had learned the unusual sound which was a combination of a woof and a soft growl and sounded for all the world like he was fussing or agreeing with her. There was no mistaking his intent.

"Yes, I know. Come on."

He pranced down the aisleway on his leash in front of her occasionally glancing back at the woman he worshiped.

Reg, Haven, and Elizabeth also got up and followed the pair out of the car.

Bone and Loraine went out the opposite door.

"Feels good to walk a bit, doesn't it, babe?"

Loraine glanced up at him. "Got a feeling we're going to wish we were back on the railroad soon."

He grinned. "Got a point."

Reg headed inside the depot after he had disembarked.

Silke and Elizabeth walked Bear Dog over to a grassy area with several still bare small oaks that had been planted by the railroad. He sniffed around several places before taking care of his business.

"How come the train doesn't go to Santa Fe, Silke? It's named the Santa Fe railroad, idn't it?"

"Well, actually, no, honey, this one is the Fort Worth and Denver Railway…You probably heard your daddy mention the Atchison, Topeka and Santa Fe…It does go into Santa Fe, New Mexico, but from Kansas…way to the north…Understand?"

She nodded. "I think so."

"I'm sure that one day this railroad will go all the way from Texas to Santa Fe an' beyond…just not yet."

Reg Berkley approached Bone and Loraine standing out on the platform as he walked out of the depot with a newspaper under his arm.

He held out his hand. "Deputy Bone, my name is Reg Berkley and I was talking with Silke on the train…"

Bone nodded and shook his proffered hand. "Saw you, just couldn't hear the conversation over the noise of the car clacking over the rails."

"I'm sure. Be that as it may…she said I should speak to you…I also am traveling to Santa Fe for business and would feel much safer if we were to travel together across the *Llano Estacado*."

Bone studied the well-dressed man for a moment and glanced at Loraine. "I'm sure that could be arranged. You would have to have your own supplies. We only have enough for the five of us and our stock."

"Yes, quite right. Quite right…I had planned to get a pack animal and supplies in Childress. My own horse is already loaded in the livestock car."

"We're spending the night in Childress an' will get an early start in the morning…Just be ready when we are…Oh…are you armed?"

"Yes, I have a long gun with my gear. Planned on hunting some along the way to supplement my supplies."

"See you in Childress, then." He touched the brim of his hat.

Bone and Loraine watched as the man strolled back to the car and boarded.

He looked down at her. "Wonder why he didn't mention the shoulder holster gun he had under his jacket?"

Loraine nodded. "Wondered that myself."

The conductor ambled along the side of the passenger cars. "Board! All aboard…Vernon, Chillicothe, Quanah an' Childress…All aboard!"

§§§

CHAPTER SEVEN

CHILDRESS, TEXAS

The bib overall clad hostler for the Fort Worth and Denver Railway led Bone's big Hildebrandt, a black half Friesian, down the cleated ramp from the livestock car first. He and his assistant had tacked the animals just after the train stopped for what was temporarily the end of the line.

The assistant, a young half Comanche lad around seventeen, brought Loraine's Sweet Face sorrel mare next.

The two men alternated until all the stock had been unloaded, including Berkley's blood bay gelding, and Ted, the pack mule.

Berkley walked up and took the reins to his horse and turned to Bone. "Where are you folks staying for tonight?"

"I understand there's only one place in town, the Dwight Hotel." Bone looked at the hostler. "There a livery close to the hotel, pard?"

"Shore is…Harrison's Stable an' Livery…right next door. Gives a discount fer folks astayin' at the hotel, too…They's Sally's Restaurant on t'other side…some larapin good eatin'. An' the Red River Saloon is 'cross the street."

Berkley smiled. "Sounds like everything's in walking distance then."

"Ah-yep…could say." The hostler checked the panniers on Ted. "Yer ready to go."

Bone handed him two Morgan silver dollars. "Much obliged."

The wiry fifty year old looked at the coins and grinned showing his tobacco-stained teeth. “My pleasure, folks. Ya’ll have a good trip, hear?”

Everyone mounted up. Bone took the lead rope to Ted and they started off at a walk toward the hotel three blocks down the dirt street from the depot.

Haven glanced at the sparse buildings along the dirt street. “Wonder what the population is?”

Bone looked over at Haven on *d'Artagnan* beside him. “I’m gonna guess a bit less than fifteen hundred people…”

He glanced at a large windmill on the left side of the street as they passed it with the nine tin blades rotating in the breeze. “I’d say that supplies the water for the town and the railroad…Don’t see another…This whole area of the *Llano Estacado* and all the way up to South Dakota is supplied by the Ogallala Aquifer. It ranges from twenty feet under the ground up to around four hundred…Understand that much of the water comes from glaciers up in Canada.”

Silke glanced at him. “Really? That’s facinatin’. Looks so dry on top to have all that water underneath.”

They reined up in front of the large green barn type structure with two large double doors in the middle of the front. A rail-thin man in dungarees walked out of the open aisleway, leaned a four-tined pitchfork against the door on his right and hitched his suspenders.

"How do?...Name's Ben Harrison...like our President, no relation though...Don't think."

Bone nodded. "Ben. Got room for our stock? Only going to be here one night."

"Stayin' at the Dwight?"

"We are."

"Be a dollar a head with grain...seventy-five cents without."

"We'll take the with."

"Alight then, I'll untack an' give 'em a groomin' fer yuh. They'll be ready at daylight."

Silke looked down at Bear Dog. "You want to come with us or stay with Ted?"

He pranced on both front feet, jumped up, turned around in the air and sat down next to Ted's big front hooves.

Ben grinned. "Looks like that's yer answer, Missy."

"I'd say…He's got some kind of connection with that mule…I'll bring you some meat an' bones from the restaurant."

Bear Dog *woo-wooed* at her and spun around again.

The hostler laughed. "Talks, too, don't he?"

Bone chuckled. "Don't get him started, he'll monopolize the conversation…Not one to argue with either."

"Watch my step."

They dismounted, removed their carpet bags, rifles, and saddlebags and headed toward the hotel next door.

They registered for two rooms, Bone and Loraine in one and Silke, Haven, and Elizabeth in the other across the hall upstairs.

Silke reached for one of the keys. "Ya'll want to meet at Sally's after we get settled in?"

Loraine grinned. "Thought you'd never bring it up…since Bone ate all the sandwiches on the way an' all but one slice of cake." She punched him in the side.

"Ow…Always pickin' on me."

"To coin one of your own sayings, my dear…If the shoe fits, throw it at the wall."

He frowned. "Why do I say that?"

Loraine looked askance at him. "Why do you say most things?"

Silke shook her head at the couple. "Meet ya'll back here in 'bout five minutes?" She looked down at Elizabeth. "You hungry, honey?"

She glanced at Bone, and smiled. "Uh-huh."

"Works for us." Bone nodded as he grabbed his and Loraine's gear and headed up the stairs.

She glanced at Silke, Haven, and Elizabeth as she followed him. "I'm so lucky."

Reg Berkley stepped up to the counter after waiting his turn to register.

Five minutes later Haven, Elizabeth, and Silke came back down the stairs to join Bone and Loraine already there with Berkley.

"You must be hungry, Bone."

Loraine slipped her arm through his elbow. "He's always hungry, Silke…After ya'll." She tilted her head to the door.

The six people ambled out, then down the duck board walk to Sally's next door.

Berkley opened the nine foot tall, half glass door, and stood back to allow the others to enter first.

Haven held Elizabeth's hand and was first through. "Thank you, Mister Berkley."

He nodded and closed the door after everyone had entered.

They paused to smell the enticing odors of fried chicken, grilled steaks, and fresh apple pie wafting in the air.

Silke sniffed. "Oh, my, if I weren't already hungry, I would be now."

Elizabeth grinned. "Me too."

A somewhat stout woman with her hair up in a bun and in an ankle length gray day dress walked up. "Evenin' folks, I'm Sally. Ya'll follow me, got just the table for you."

She led them to a larger round table near the center of the fifty by fifty foot room.

"Ya'll have a seat…Now, special tonight is fried chicken, smashed taters an' milk gravy, put-by green beans, an' hot yeast rolls. We also got pan steaks an' Irish stew…'course if your nose works, you know I've got fresh an' hot apple pie."

Bone looked up from his chair. "Yes."

Sally's forehead wrinkled. "Yes?"

Loraine shook her head and thumped Bone's shoulder.

"Ow."

"He's being a smart-alec, Sally, meaning he wants all of it."

The hefty woman laughed. "Well, honey, if that's what he wants he can sure have it."

"He'll have the special as will I."

Bone shrugged his big shoulders—a sheepish grin on his face.

"Good for me, too." Silke looked at Elizabeth.

"Uh-huh, please an' thank you."

Haven grinned. "Put me on the list, too."

Berkley nodded. "Just as well make it all the way around, Ma'am."

"Six specials comin' up…Coffee, tea, sweet milk or buttermilk."

"Can I have sweet milk, Ma'am?"

"What's your name, honey?"

"Lizbeth."

"Well, you certainly can, Lizbeth…Bet that's short for Elizabeth, idn't it?"

She nodded. "Yes, Ma'am."

Sally leaned over close to Elizabeth. "Would you like chocolate sweet milk?"

Elizabeth bounced in her seat. "Oh, yes, Ma'am, please." She glanced at Silke with a big grin. "I love chocolate sweet milk."

"And how 'bout the grownups?"

Bone raised his eyebrows. "Chocolate milk?"

"Bone?" Loraine thumped him again.

He took a deep breath and sighed. "Coffee, Ma'am."

The others nodded.

"Five coffees an' one big chocolate sweet milk." Sally winked at Elizabeth, turned and walked toward the kitchen.

Silke looked at Berkley sitting next to Haven. "You're certainly familiar, Reg, have we met somewhere before the train?"

"Oh, I don't think so, Silke. I only came into Gainesville yesterday…from Oklahoma City, Topeka, Kansas, and Denver, Colorado, before that."

Silke frowned and shook her head. "I just know I've seen you somewhere…can't place it. Maybe it'll come to me."

LLANO ESTACADO

Four rough looking gunhawks trotted their horses southwest toward the cattle town of Blue Water (later renamed Hereford) from Amarillo, a distance of some forty-eight miles.

The leader, a large man known as Mad Jack Kercher, had a white scar on the side of his face from the corner of his right eye down to his jaw line in front of his ear…the result of a knife fight with a half-breed. The other man wasn't so fortunate.

"What'n hell makes this job so urgent, Jack?"

Kercher turned his milky eye to his underling. "Luke, you're dumber'n a *bois d' arc* stump. What's ever job we've done been about?"

"Uh…Money?"

"Damn, your mama have any kids that lived?"

"Huh?…Shore, I got a brother…Hey, yer funnin' at me, ain'tcha?"

"You figger it out…For you other numb-nuts, this is gonna be the biggest haul we've ever had."

§§§

CHAPTER EIGHT

SALLY'S RESTAURANT

"Well, dang, that was some kind of good." Bone pushed back from the table. "Anybody for going across the street for a beer?" He looked at Elizabeth. "All but you, little bit."

She giggled. "I know…beer's just for you grownups."

Haven smiled. "I think I fit in your category, too, Lizbeth…I'm only eighteen. Why don't you an' I go to our room an' I just happen to have a deck of cards…Bet I can beat you at 'Slapjack'…How's that?"

"Betcha can't, Haven…But I'm better at Black Jack."

"How do you know 'bout Black Jack?"

"Unka Mack taught me…He owned a saloon, you know?"

Haven, Silke, Bone, and Loraine exchanged glances and smiles.

"Now, you own a saloon, Lizbeth." Silke looked at her. She glanced at Berkley. "She inherited the Painted Lady Saloon in Gainesville from one of her uncles, Reg."

"My, that's very nice. I'm in the company of a *boni fide* business woman." He smiled at her.

"Oh! That's right, I forgot. Padrino's takin' care of it for me while we're gone…Hope he's doin' it right."

Everyone chuckled.

Bone patted her shoulder. "Think you can count on that, hon. My Padrino can do most anything he sets his mind to. He was a war hero, you know?"

"He is? A real hero? Wow!"

"And, fact is, he taught me how to play poker, Black Jack, and Faro, when I was about your age…Not to mention chess, too."

"Oh! I love chess. Wish we had a board."

"Maybe your grandmother has one," suggested Loraine as she too got up from the table.

Silke also got to her feet and hugged Elizabeth. "We'll see you back at the room in a bit…Don't take all of Haven's money."

She grinned and looked over at Haven. "I'll be nice."

Bone and Berkley both walked over to the counter and paid their bills, then joined the others as they walked out the door.

RED RIVER SALOON

Berkley held one of the batwing doors open for Silke, Loraine, and Bone. He followed behind as they strolled up to the polished bar in the saloon lit by a large wagon wheel suspended from the fourteen foot ceiling in the center with eight kerosene lamps. There were also lamps mounted around on the walls.

Loraine wrinkled her nose as she turned to Silke. "Ever notice all saloons smell like smoke, stale beer, vomit, and urine?"

Silke smiled and nodded. "More often than I care to admit."

The balding, portly bartender in a boiled white collarless shirt with red suspenders and arm garters looked up from drying some just washed four ounce gill glasses. "Evenin' folks, what'll it be?"

Bone glanced down. "Ladies."

Loraine nudged Silke. "You go first."

She nodded. "Got *Herradura* tequila?"

"Yessum."

It was Loraine's turn. "Lone Star beer for me."

"Make that two," said Bone.

"I'll have *Courvoisier Cognac*, if you have it."

The bartender nodded at Berkley. "Napoleon's favorite…of course." He turned, got two Lone Stars from his zinc lined cooler, wiped the water from them and set them on the bar followed by two of the heavy gill glasses he had just dried. "Don't have no brandy glasses, mister…not much call for 'em."

"A gill glass will be fine." Reg put two silver dollars on the bar. "First round's on me."

Bone grinned as he picked up his bottle of Lone Star and flipped the wire loop holding the ceramic top on the bottle up and pushed it to the side. "I got the next."

A smallish, ruddy-faced man in a garish plaid suit behind Bone spoke up in an Irish brogue, "Aye, man-mountain, if it's drinks ye be buyin', it's the polite thing to include the rest of us standin' here at the bar."

Bone looked down at the 5'6" tall drummer. "Well, little man, be glad to…long as the next one is on you."

The man set his drink down, blew out his chest and thrust it toward Bone, bumping him slightly. "An' it's takin' offense, I am, at bein' called 'little man'. I'll be thankin' ye to take it back or I'll have to be thumpin' ye…Ye big gorilla."

Loraine leaned around Bone. "Probably be a good idea, mister, to back off and leave well enough alone."

"An' who be ye, woman? His sugar tit keeper?"

Bone rolled his eyes. "Oh, boy…Mistake." He glanced down at Loraine and shook his head.

"Wonder why it is, babe, it's the little bitty guys always act like a banty rooster and think they're the baddest thing in the forest?"

The drummer with a dark green bowler cocked on his head poked Bone in the chest with his finger. "Is it me ye're referrin' to as 'little bitty'?...Ye *Fomóire* clansman."

Bone glanced at Loraine. "What's a *Fomóire*?"

Silke grinned and spoke up, "Irish nether giants...malevolent spirits dwelling underwater and in the nether regions of the earth."

"Do I look malevolent?...Don't answer that." He turned back to the drummer. "Why don't you do what my wife suggested and leave well enough alone?"

"Ye got a wife, ye big ox?...She must be daft, to be married to such as ye." He poked Bone again.

"Oh, what the hell?"

Bone brought his ham-like fist over his head and down on the top of the little man's bowler in a hammer blow, crushing it down to his ears. The Irishman's eyes rolled back in his head as he dropped to the plank floor like a pile of wet newspapers.

Loraine peeked around Bone again and down at the drummer crumpled at his feet. “Some guys just have to learn the hard way…I warned him.”

Bone turned to the bartender and pitched a silver dollar on the bar. “Pour him whatever he’s drinking when he wakes up.”

“You got it, big man.”

“You shouldn’t oughta hit that little feller, man mountain.”

An inebriated cowboy sitting at a nearby table with three others reached for the Colt on his hip only to have the pointed end of Silke’s tomahawk pin his shirt sleeve to the arm of the bow chair he was sitting in with an audible thunk as she threw it from eight feet away.

He looked down at the Chickasaw war hatchet embedded in the oak chair through the material of his shirt less than a quarter inch from his hand. The color drained from his weathered, stubbled face as he quickly sobered up—his eyes slowly tracked up to her grinning face.

“That could have just as easily been in your hand, cowboy.” She stepped over and pulled the deadly weapon free, stuck the top of the blade under his chin and lifted up. “Now why don’t you turn back around to your card game an' the who-hit-John, an' mind your own business?"

He looked at her still smiling face, then at the hand cannon on her hip. "Yessum, believe I will."

The little drummer staggered to his feet assisting himself by holding on to the bar. When he was finally standing, he grabbed both sides of his bowler and pushed up. The stiff round-topped hat made a popping sound as it came free from his head full of carrot-colored hair. He set his hat back on his head at a rakish angle as before.

He shook his head and blinked several times. "What it was that ye hit me with, big man?"

Bone glanced down from his 6'8" height. "A sample…Just be glad I didn't sic my sweet bride on you or our attractive friend here…They'd of hurtcha."

"Faith an' begorrah, it's like bein' a sham to ye, yer missus an' the other lady, I'd like to be."

"Sham?"

"Aye, it's an Irish word for friend…Me name is Mickalene." He stuck out his hand.

Bone enveloped the proffered hand in his massive mitt. "Well, I think that's good, pard…My friends, and enemies far as that goes, call me

Bone." He glanced at the bar as the bartender set a gill of Irish whiskey in front of Mickalene.

He picked up the glass and held it out. Bone did the same with his bottle of Lone Star.

"May ye be in heaven a full half-hour before the devil knows you're dead."

Bone nodded and grinned. "Works for me."

Mickalene downed his double shot as Bone chugged his beer.

Berkley glanced at Silke with more than a little admiration. "Where did you learn to handle a tomahawk like that?"

She smiled as she slipped it back into the beaded belt around her doeskin clad shapely hips below her tiny waist—the belt also held her holstered Smith and Wesson 500, .50 caliber pistol.

"I worked with a Chickasaw Lighthorse for two years, *Nashoba Hommá*...Red Wolf, up in the Nations. He taught me how to handle a tomahawk...among other things." She showed him her pure silver crossed tomahawk necklace. "I'm a member of the Chickasaw Nation Hatchet Woman Clan...It's a division of the Warrior Class. I was presented this by their head Shaman, *Anompoli Lawa*...translated, means, He Who Talks to Many."

"Really? The Chickasaw have women warriors?"

"They do, indeed. Two categories…the Panther Woman Clan is responsible for strategy and communications, an' the Hatchet Woman Clan that actually participate in the battles…I was inducted a few months ago an' was presented with this totem." She held out the necklace.

"My, my…You are an unusual woman."

LLANO ESTACADO

Mad Jack Kercher held up his hand as they waded up on the bank after crossing the belly-deep water of Tule Creek. "Camp here. Got water an' graze…Luke, you hobble the horses after you water 'em. J.D. why don't you gather up some good dry driftwood an' git a fire started."

"Who do you want cookin' tonight, Jack?" Ace Cole stepped down from his dun gelding and started unwrapping his latigo.

"Well, since you brung it up, it can be your turn tonight."

J.D. looked over as he pulled his tack. "Durn, Jack, Ace even burns water."

Kercher chuckled. "You can cook well as build the fire…You've a mind, Burdick."

The skinny as a whip outlaw frowned. "I cain't cook much better."

Jack unrolled his tan ground tarp, then his blankets. "'Nuff said."

"When we s'posed to be in Blue Water, Jack?" Luke asked from the creek as he watered the horses for the evening.

"Got plenty time…Day after tomorrow."

J.D. Burdick looked up from building his tinder pile in the fire pit he had constructed by ringing some rocks. "Gonna be 'ny killin'?"

Mad Jack leaned back against his saddle and cut a plug from his twist of tobacco with his Bowie. "You know how the boss is 'bout witnesses."

§§§

CHAPTER NINE

DWIGHT HOTEL

Haven and Elizabeth sat on the patchwork quilt that covered one of the beds in their hotel room, talking.

"When did your cousin, Maggie, give you all those pearls, Lizbeth?"

"Right before we left Caddo Lake to go to Gainesville."

"Why didn't she come?"

"On account she was dead."

Haven frowned. "You mean she got killed after she gave you the pearls?"

Elizabeth shook her head. "Uh-uh…She died two years ago…the bad men chased her into the lake an' she drowned tryin' to get away."

"I don't understand, then how did she give you the pearls?"

"She gave Silke, Bone, an' them one each. A blue one for the boys an' a wine colored one for the girls…like the one I'm givin' grandma…an' then tol' 'em there was bunches more at the house…I'd been playin' with 'em as marbles."

"But, I still don't understand how she gave Silke an' the others pearls if she was dead?"

"I didn't see her, but Bone, Loraine, Silke, Padrino, Marshal Farmer, an' the teenagers from Gainesville stayin' on Horse Island did. They talked to her a lot."

Haven shook her head. "How did they talk to her if she died two years ago?…This is not makin' any sense, sweetheart."

Elizabeth sat up on the bed and put her fists on her hips. "She came back to help get rid of the bad men. Maggie was there several days an' helped kill some of 'em...Silke said she saw her, Unka Mack an' Unka James all holdin' hands watchin' us leave when we left to go back to Jefferson."

"You mean they were ghosts?"

"They were real...least Maggie was. Everbody but me talked to her...She came back to help...Silke said Bear Dog liked her, too...an' he doesn't just like anybody."

Haven fell back on one of the pillows. "Oh, my...Wow! I've heard of such things..."

There was a tap on the door, then it opened—Silke stepped inside as Bone and Loraine went into their room across the hall and Berkley down the hall to his.

"Ya'll are still up?" Silke unbuckled her beaded belt and laid it along with her gun, Bowie knife, and tomahawk on the dresser next to her bed.

Haven nodded. "We've been talkin'. Lizbeth was tellin' me about Maggie...an' that she was dead."

"It's all true. We were with her a lot, 'specially when we were fightin' the shiners."

"Shiners?"

Silke pursed her lips. "A large clan…fifteen or so…of inbred moonshiners that practiced cannibalism…among other things." Her eyes flicked toward Elizabeth. "If you know what I mean."

Haven nodded she understood.

"They killed one of the teen boys an' almost one of the girls before we rescued her."

"Oooh, yuk…How awful."

"Maggie an' her uncles, Timothy an' James helped us wipe 'em out…They were killed in the fight."

"I'm so sorry, Lizbeth…I really am." Haven sat up and hugged the little girl.

Elizabeth nodded. "Thank you. I really miss them." Her cornflower blue eyes started to fill as she bit her lower lip.

Silke sat down on her bed. "We had no idea that Maggie was a supernatural being until after she disappeared when we took care of the shiners an' Lizbeth told us she had drowned two years earlier."

Elizabeth wiped her eyes with the back of her knuckles. "But, her, Unka Mack, an' Unka James are happy now that ya'll sent those awful people to the bad place…I know they are."

Silke got up, stepped over to their bed, sat down on the other side of Elizabeth and hugged her. "I know they are, too, honey…I know they are, too."

SALLY'S RESTAURANT

Bone finished his plate of steak and eggs, wiped his mouth with his napkin, waved at Sally, and held up his heavy white ceramic mug.

Sally nodded, went into the kitchen and came right back out with her large blue merle graniteware coffee pot. She refilled Bone's cup and looked around the table.

"Anyone else?"

Loraine and Berkley both nodded and Sally refilled theirs also.

She looked down at Elizabeth. "How were those flapjacks, honey?"

"Oh, they were so yummy, thank you! The syrup was extra good."

"That was some sorghum made right here in Childress…Would ya'll like a can to take with you?"

A big grin spread across Bone's face. "Absolutely, Ma'am…Nothing much better than sorghum an' butter mopped up with a biscuit."

"Oh, Sally, I've got a big, almost grown, half wolf over at the livery, do you have any meat scraps an' bones I could take him?"

"Oh, goodness yes, Silke, I'll wrap some up in butcher paper…Got quite a bit from all the T-bones an' ham steaks I served this mornin'."

Loraine grinned. "Most left from what Bone ordered, I would imagine."

Sally returned her smile. "Quite a bit more than that…Do love to watch a man eat, though."

Bone took a sip of his coffee. "Just a growin' boy."

"I'm not letting out those pants anymore, mister. That buckskin is too hard to work with." Loraine poked his waist.

"There's a lot of give to leather, babe."

"It's a good thing."

Berkley glanced at the buckskin outfits Silke, Loraine, and Bone were wearing. "Interesting that ya'll are all wearing pretty much the same type of trail clothes...Even the same beading."

"Bone's grea...uh...grandmother, Deputy US Marshal Fiona Miller Flynn had her grandmother, a Cherokee up in the Nations, make them up for us...Marshal Reeves suggested they're much better on the trail, along with these tall Apache style moccasins, than regular clothing and boots," said Loraine.

"I've got to get me a set when we get back. They do look a lot more comfortable," commented Haven.

Bone nodded. "'Specially the moccasins, kiddo...if you got to do any walkin' at all."

Berkley smiled. "I would imagine."

"I should think that there's some Indians in Santa Fe that could make a pair for you, Reg, an' you, too, Haven."

"You're probably right, Silke...Oh, I never asked, where does Elizabeth's grandmother live in Santa Fe?"

"Actually, she's on a ranch south of town, the Bar M. We'll have to get directions when we get there...I'm sure the sheriff or someone will know."

Berkley nodded. "Pretty country down that way, been through there a couple of years back."

"Think she raises horses." Silke looked at Elizabeth. "Isn't that right, hon?"

"Uh-huh. That's what my Unka Mack said."

Haven cocked her eyebrow. "You have another uncle besides the ones you mentioned, Timothy and James?"

"Their last name is McPherson, she just called her uncle Timothy, Uncle Mack because she couldn't say McPherson when she was little. Isn't that right, Lizabeth?"

She looked up at Silke. "Uh-huh."

Sally came back from the kitchen with a large package wrapped in brown butcher paper, tied with string, and a quart can of sorghum. She handed the package to Silke and the can to Bone.

"Here you are, the meat and bones should last him a day or two."

Silke grinned as she got to her feet. "I don't know, Sally, he can put away a whole deer haunch in pretty short order…but thank you, this should help a lot."

"You're certainly welcome…Ya'll be sure to stop in when you come back through, you hear?"

Bone pushed his chair back. "We'll certainly do that. This has been the best eatin' since I left home."

Loraine nudged him. "Better not let Faye hear you say that."

"Oh, yeah…mum's the word." He drew his finger across his mouth.

They went out the door and stepped next door to the hotel.

Their bags were stacked beside the desk.

Bone nodded at the clerk. "Thanks for watchin' our stuff, pard."

"Not a problem, Mister Bone."

"Mister Bone was my daddy, most call me just plain Bone."

Loraine looked askance at him. "Among other things."

"Yeah, that too." He slung his saddlebags over his shoulder and picked up his carpet bag with one hand and his Marlin .45-70, lever action rifle with the other.

Everyone also grabbed their bags and long guns and they headed over to Harrison's Stable and Livery next door.

Harrison stepped out of the aisleway followed by Bear Dog. "Mornin' folks. Seen you go into Sally's this mornin' an' I went ahead an' tacked yer mounts an' loaded Ted up fer ya…That's some mule, tell you that. Had to talk right nice 'fore his buddy there would let me near 'im."

Bear Dog first looked at Berkley, curling his lip ever so slightly, then he started prancing on his front paws, spinning in a circle, finally raising up on both back feet and walking to Silke to smell the package under her arm.

"Yes, big dog, you know what I got, don't you?"

He *woo-wooed* at her, spun around again and sat down as she unwrapped it. She held up a large scrap of meat and fat. "What do you say?"

"Woof!"

"Just one?"

"Woof…woof."

"That's better." Silke pitched it at him. He caught it in the air, chewed several times and swallowed it, mostly whole.

Elizabeth put one hand to her almost nonexistent hip and wagged a finger at him. "You need to chew your food better, Bear Dog, hear me?"

He fussed back at her with his *woo* sound.

"I mean it, now."

Bear Dog ducked his head.

Silke fished into the package. "Here's another. You can have some more when we stop on down the trail…There's some bones, too."

Silke pitched another chunk of meat at him. He also caught that one—looked at Elizabeth, laid down with the scrap held between his paws and chewed on it before swallowing it in pieces.

"Good boy." Silke stepped over to Ted and put her and Elizabeth's bags in one of the panniers. She slung her saddlebags behind her cantle on *Lakná*, tied them down, and then tied her soogan on top.

The others followed suit as Bone and Berkley settled up their accounts with the hostler. Bone tipped him an extra two dollars.

"Much obliged, folks. Ya'll have a safe trip."

Bone stepped up into Hildebrandt's saddle. "Well, folks, as they say on *Rawhide*, let's head 'em up an' move 'em out."

Silke lifted Elizabeth up into Calico's saddle. "What does Bone mean, Silke?"

"With him, honey, I don't think even God really knows."

§§§

CHAPTER TEN

NORTH TEXAS

Bone, leading Ted behind him, led the way from Childress, northwest the eight miles to Prairie Dog Town Fork of the Red River. Elizabeth and Silke rode beside him with Loraine, Haven, and Reg following behind them.

The countryside was rugged, rolling hills of prairie grass—bluestem, Indian grass, grama, and buffalo grass—along with scattered mesquite and cedar trees. The occasional stream-cut gullies were lined with post oak, pecan, sycamore, and cottonwood trees. Some of the mesquite were thirty to forty feet high and around the same in diameter.

Bear Dog ran alongside the group for a while, stopped and marked a bush, or smelled some coon or bobcat scat.

Bone turned to Elizabeth. "Be sure you stay well away from those mesquite trees, honey." He pointed to one next to the trail. "The new growth this time of year has some real ouchy thorns…Won't do you or Calico much good."

She looked at the light green foliage covered tree. "Oh, I didn't know, Bone…Calico an' I thank you."

Silke squeezed *Lakná* up even with Bone. "How far is it to Blue Water?"

"Accordin' to the map I got at the hotel, looks like a little over a hundred miles. We gotta track alongside the river through the Palo Duro Canyon to the South *Cita* Creek…then follow it west to Blue Water."

Haven trotted up next to them at the front. “Ya’ll know the Palo Duro is the second largest canyon in North America after the Grand Canyon in Arizona?”

“Understand the Comanche used to hide out in there before Colonel Ranald, Bad Hand, Mackenzie slaughtered most of their horse herd and sent the tribe up to Lawton,” added Bone.

“Why was he called ‘Bad Hand’,” asked Elizabeth.

Bone glanced at her. “He lost the first two fingers of his right hand during Lincoln’s war and the Indians gave him the nickname of ‘Bad Hand’ or sometimes ‘No Finger Chief’.”

“That’s interesting.”

Loraine moved up behind Bone. “Remember Bodie Hickman said to keep an eye out. He’d heard of some Comanche and Kiowa renegades plus a few owlhoots still hanging out in there.”

Berkley glanced over at her. “Who’s Bodie Hickman?”

“Oh, I’m sorry, Reg. Texas Ranger Bodie Hickman…He and his wife are close friends back in Gainesville…Fact is, we live at the same boarding house.”

"Ah, I see. Thank you. Probably good advice if it's from a Ranger...Say, Bone, how far is it to the canyon?"

"I make it about another six miles to the river, Reg...'bout an hour at this pace...We'll water the stock when we get to the river. Be a couple miles from the mouth of the canyon to the west...That'll keep them till we camp this evening."

Bone turned to Loraine. "Hey, babe, come up here and take good ol' Ted's lead rope. I'm going to ride ahead on point for a bit. Not real familiar with this country."

She trotted Sweet Face up beside Bone as he unwrapped the lead dally from his saddle horn, took it from him, and dallied off on her own. "Got it."

He squeezed Hildebrandt up into a road trot and soon disappeared over the top of the next hill—Bear Dog loped with that long-legged, mile eating stride of a wolf right behind them occasionally cutting his blue eyes off to the right at a ridge.

On the other side of the hill, a ten foot deep wash ran parallel to the narrow road, Bone turned sharply down a game cut in the side right after passing a large juniper. Once at the bottom, he pulled up and looked down at Bear Dog.

"Don't know if you noticed, old son, but we had some eyes on us."

Bear Dog spun around and a low growl rumbled from deep in his throat.

"Oh, you saw 'em, huh?…What say we slip up toward that ridge and take a gander at whoever it is?"

He spun around again and trotted off up the draw in the direction of the rocky ridge—Bone and Hildebrandt followed behind.

They followed the gully several hundred yards until Bone reined up again. "This should be good enough, boy."

He dismounted, ground tied Hildebrandt, and checked his S & W 500 and his combat knife. They struck out on foot, climbed the side of the draw, and Bone stuck his head above the lip from behind a juniper. Bear Dog belly-crawled up beside him and laid down.

They peered through the dark green foliage at the top of the ridge. Bone could make out a hatless man with long black hair confined by a red headband, watching the road behind and below him with field glasses.

"Indian, Bear Dog. Probably one of those renegades Bodie mentioned. He's watching the others coming along the trail…Not good. Bet he's not alone…scouting for his friends." He glanced down at the wolf dog's blue eyes looking back at him. "Get 'im, Bear Dog."

The big hybrid canine crawled over the top of the lip of the ridge and zigzagged through the brush to the side of the incline. He crested the top of the ridge to the right of the renegade and charged.

Bear Dog hit the prone buckskin clad Indian at full speed. The force of the impact rolled the man over several times and Bear Dog hit him again, grabbing his right forearm in the process as he raised it up to protect his face and throat.

Shrill screams split the quiet midday air, combined with deep snarls and growls from Bear Dog as he worried the Indian's arm.

The swarthy complexioned renegade managed to struggle to his feet. He slung Bear Dog to the side, ripping half of his leather sleeve off as the eighty pound animal rolled down the front incline of the ridge—he stopped at the bottom.

The Indian's bloody arm hung limply, his hand twisted at an odd angle, as he disappeared down the other side.

Bear Dog jumped to his feet and sprinted back up the side of the ridge.

"Bear Dog, that's enough," Bone commanded as he heard hoofbeats galloping off.

He crawled over the edge of the arroyo, jogged to the ridge and climbed up the slope to meet Bear Dog at the top. The faithful animal held the bloody buckskin sleeve of the Indian's shirt in his mouth—Bone took it from him.

"Good boy." He patted the top of his broad head as he looked at the torn leather. "If he's right handed, not going to be using that arm much for a spell, I would think."

Bone stepped over where the Indian had lain and picked up the abandoned field glasses where he dropped them when Bear Dog hit him. He walked over to where the man had tethered his horse and knelt down to study the tracks.

"Yep, unshod…Where there's one, gonna be more. What do you think, boy?"

Bear Dog *woo-wooed* low back at Bone.

"Yeah, me too…Let's get back to the others."

They worked their way down the slope of the ridge to the draw and back to where Hildebrandt was ground tied.

Ten minutes later they trotted up to the group. Loraine pulled rein on Sweet Face, and stopped Ted.

Bone held up the tattered and bloody buckskin sleeve. "Had an admirer…Bear Dog wanted to play with him but he decided he had other places he needed to be after his arm was torn up and most likely broken…I can tell you this, Bear Dog is kinda scary when he's on the prod."

"Could've told you that…Renegade?"

Bone glanced at Silke. "My guess…Think he was scouting us out for his pals. Dollar to a donut they're planning an ambush somewhere in the Palo Duro."

Silke nodded. "Be a lot of places…what Bodie said."

A concerned Berkley looked at Bear Dog, then at the torn bloody sleeve. "Now what, Bone?"

Bone grinned. "We let 'em."

"Excuse me?"

"This country is a whole lot like Afghanistan. I fought the Taliban there when I was in the Marine Corps…Kind of used to it."

Berkley looked puzzled. "I didn't know America was fighting over there."

Bone caught himself. "Oh, uh…just a little clean up of President Jefferson's previous action against the Muslims on the Barbary Coast."

"Really?"

"Believe it."

Berkley still looked puzzled. "So, what do you have in mind?"

"Well, how about you lead the pack mule and stay with Silke, Haven, and Elizabeth…Loraine'll drop back and cover our six, Bear Dog and I'll take point again."

"Our six what?" Berkley wasn't following Bone.

"Uh, that's military speak for covering our backsides."

"Oh."

"Don't you want me to ride up on point with you?" asked Silke.

"Nope, ya'll need to stay together so you can cover Elizabeth…I've done this before. They won't see me unless I want them to." He grinned again. "This is what I do."

He turned back to Loraine. "You all right with covering our six, babe?"

"Piece of cake."

"Be sure to ride off to the side of their trail, keep in the brush as much as you can and back about a hundred yards."

"I know, Bone."

"Everbody check your weapons…That gun in the shoulder holster you got there, too, Berkley."

Reg's eyes widened.

"Yeah, saw it the first time we met on the train. What is it, a Webly Bulldog?"

"Uh, yes, but how…"

"I'm a cop, Berkley…I see things like that…A .44 caliber, right?"

"Yes, it is."

"Only got an effective range of about fifteen yards. Better carry your rifle across your lap."

"Uh, right. Good idea."

Bone rolled his big black gelding to the side as he and Bear Dog trotted off toward the mouth of the Palo Duro, working their way into the cottonwood, sycamore, and willows that grew along the river banks.

Loraine turned back the way they came and disappeared into the brush.

Silke glanced at Berkley. “Shall we, Reg?”

He nodded and bumped his blood bay gelding lightly in the ribs, leading Ted off behind him along the sandy trail that ran beside the river.

“You follow Mister Berkley, Lizbeth…are you scared?”

She looked back at Silke. “Uh-uh…Got you, Haven, Bone, an’ Loraine watching out for me.”

“Nothing wrong with being scared, honey…Nothing wrong with it at all. Just remember to do what I ask of you without hesitation…Do you understand?”

Elizabeth smiled, nodded and kicked Calico up into a trot to catch up with Berkley…

§§§

CHAPTER ELEVEN

PALO DURO CANYON

Bone trotted Hildebrandt the two miles to the wide mouth of the canyon. He reined over into a copse of cedar another half mile inside that opened into a small clearing in the middle.

"Looks like there's a little grazing in here for you, pal. Gonna leave you here and go on foot."

Bone dismounted, loosened the girth, and ground tied the big gelding.

"Be back in a bit, you're too big and will make more noise than I need. Plus, I can move ahead of the group just as fast and get up a little higher so, Bear Dog and I can scout things out…Know you don't understand what I'm saying…"

Hildebrandt turned his big brown eyes at Bone and blinked twice.

"Hmm…then again, maybe you do."

He patted the half Friesian gelding on his thick, muscular neck, grabbed a drink from his canteen and hung it back on his saddlehorn.

"Let's go, Bear Dog."

Together, they slipped off through the cedar brush that gave the area a fresh clean smell, into the canyon proper at a jog working their way up the side.

Berkley glanced somewhat nervously at the rising cliffs on both sides of the river. The average six mile wide canyon was one hundred twenty miles long. It had been created by millennia of water erosion from the Prairie Dog Town Fork of the Red

River as it dramatically and suddenly ran off the Caprock Escarpment.

Elizabeth scanned the steep walls of the canyon and turned to Silke. "Those cliffs are high. How deep does the canyon get?"

Silke followed her gaze. "I'm told it's up to most of a quarter mile."

"Golly whiz! Those things up yonder..." Elizabeth pointed down the canyon. "What are they? Look almost like people standin' there."

"Called hoodoos, honey. They were carved by wind and water over many thousands of years." Silke indicated a large one in the distance. "That big one up there looks like a lighthouse at the ocean."

"I've seen pictures of those."

The rugged canyon complex area in front of them was mesmerizing and almost ethereal with multi-layered colored rock formations and boulders seemingly balanced precariously on top.

Haven shook her head. "I can see why the Indians found it a good place to hide out."

Silke nodded. "I've also been told that before the white man killed off most of the buffalo in the '70s an' '80s, that thousands of them wintered in here. There was water, grass, an' shelter from the winds."

Haven turned in her saddle. "I don't see Loraine back there."

Silke grinned. "She doesn't want you to. If we could…so could the renegades."

Sets of black eyes watched Berkley, Silke, Haven, and Elizabeth work their way along the sandy banks of the river into the heart of the canyon.

The right arm of the owner of one of the pair of eyes watching the trail was bandaged with blood soaked rags and was held to his body by a leather strap around his neck.

The eight renegades—five Comanche, and three Kiowa, exchanged glances and nods. As one, they moved back away from their vantage point to their mustangs tethered in a clump of cedars.

They mounted and worked their way single file from an area of scattered boulders that had fallen from the cliff face eons earlier down to what would later be called the Rock Garden Trail.

The leader, a small, wiry, Comanche watched from the shadow of one of the large rocks as

Berkley, leading the pack mule, led the group past their hiding place to the northwest.

As Silke, who was behind Haven, Berkley, and Elizabeth passed by the hidden Indians, the leader held up his fist until she disappeared from view around a twist in the trail.

He dropped his arm, screamed, and kicked his horse's ribs with the heels of his moccasin clad feet, "Hy-yi-yi-yi!"

The group of renegades charged out of their hiding spot almost a hundred yards behind Silke and the others, screaming, yelling, and brandishing their pistols and rifles—the leader fired his Colt.

Silke turned in her saddle at the sound of the first yell. "Berkley! Go, go, go!" She kicked *Lakná* in the sides and drew her Smith and Wesson.

Haven nudged up alongside Elizabeth. "Ride, honey, ride! Hurry…Stay with Reg…Go!" She pulled her Peacemaker from the holster as her cousin rode up beside her.

Silke shouted over the pounding of their mount's hooves, the screams of the Indians, and the first couple of shots fired in their direction, "Let Berkley and Lizbeth get a little ahead, then on my signal, we'll turn, separate, and charge the renegades."

Haven nodded as they both bumped their horses back a little.

Loraine saw the last of the Indians gallop out of their hideout up in front of her in pursuit of the girls and Berkley. She pulled her Kimber 1911A semiautomatic .45 from her holster, thumbed the safety to *off* and kicked Sweet Face up into a run.

Several hundred yards in front of Berkley, Bone heard the first sounds of the chase. He turned and sprinted back down the slope to where he had left Hildebrandt in the copse of cedar.

"Oh, damn! Go, big dog, go!"

Bear Dog quickly outdistanced the big man and headed toward where he knew his mistress was, dodging and twisting through and around the scattered cedar and mesquite.

The Comanche and Kiowa were known in the Indian wars as the finest light cavalry in the world—but these renegades were the dregs of a once proud warrior people. However, they were no less dangerous to the group they chased.

Berkley and Elizabeth increased their lead in front of Silke and Haven to almost a hundred yards.

Silke glanced at Haven. "Now!"

They both rolled their horses back, Silke to the left, Haven to the right and kicked them up to a hard gallop directly back in the face of the oncoming savages, spreading apart as they did—their weapons extended straight out from their shoulders.

Bone reached Hildebrandt, tightened the cinch, jerked the latigo down, jumped up into the saddle, reached forward under the big horse's neck, grabbed his reins, and spun the animal about. They charged in the direction of the melee.

Bear Dog was the first to reach the renegades. He sprinted toward the leader's Appaloosa and leapt at his head.

At the same time, Silke and Haven started firing their pistols at a full gallop. They could see Loraine coming up behind the Indians and adjusted their aim accordingly.

Silke's .50 cal boomed, echoing off the canyon walls, followed shortly by the smaller explosions of sound from Haven's .38-40.

Bear Dog latched onto the nose of the Appy, simultaneously as a round from Silke caught the rider in the chest blowing him backward from his saddle—dead before he hit the ground.

The red and white spotted Appy did a somersault at full gallop and tumbled forward another fifteen or twenty yards as Bear Dog danced out of the way after releasing his nose.

Loraine, also at a gallop, triggered off rapid fire shots from her .45 at the renegades from their rear as Silke and Haven poured bullets at them from the front.

Three more Indians were knocked from their saddles as Loraine, Silke, and Haven all found their targets.

The remaining four renegades panicked at the unexpected pincer fire coming at them from two directions. They turned first one way, then another, and finally scattered to both sides of the trail.

Silke fired the last 300 grain round from her 500, catching one of the Kiowa in the back of his head and exploding it in a cloud of pink mist like a ripe watermelon.

Loraine galloped up to Silke and Haven as the last three Indians disappeared into the brush—two of the three obviously wounded.

Loraine reined Sweet Face up. "Ya'll all right?"

Silke and Haven exchanged glances.

"I'm good," said Silke as Bear Dog trotted up to *Lakná*.

"Me too," added Haven as Bone loped up to the trio.

He quickly scanned the three for injuries, and then looked about at the scattered bodies which included the one with his right arm bandaged that Bear Dog was sniffing.

"Well, big dog, see you found your playmate…" He turned to the girls. "Ya'll could have left me one or two…How many got away?"

Loraine glanced at the woods. "I saw three…and two of them were bleeding…There's one out there if you want to go track him down."

"Think ya'll made your point. Damn good strategy…Who came up with that?"

The three girls looked at each other and grinned.

Silke shrugged her shoulders. "Just kinda worked out that way, Bone. Haven and I separated when we charged 'em an' then we saw Loraine comin' up from their backside, shootin'…so we adapted. Then Bear Dog took out the leader's horse the same time I shot him out of the saddle."

Bone grinned and shook his head. "Adapt…The Marine Corp credo…What ya'll did, we do in our time for recreation…Call it mounted shooting. Big difference is the balloons we shoot crushed walnut hull loaded blanks at don't shoot back."

Haven nodded. "Didn't realize you could be accurate shootin' that way, before."

Bone smiled. "Your hand doesn't move much at a full gallop…Just point and fire."

"A little trickier with a semiautomatic. Gotta go back and see if I can find the empty magazine I dropped after my first eight shots," commented Loraine.

"I'll help you, babe…Silke, ya'll go on and catch up with Berkley and Elizabeth. I passed them and told them to keep going…Slowed down some by now, I imagine. Need to rest these animals."

She nodded. "Good idea. Come on Haven."

They trotted their lathered mounts back the way they had come.

Bear Dog stayed with Bone and Loraine. His head was cocked with concern as he looked at Loraine.

"You look a little peaked, honey, you all right?"

Loraine raised her arm and showed him the splotch of blood staining her doeskin top on her side under her arm…

§§§

CHAPTER TWELVE

BAR M RANCH
NEW MEXICO

A trim, gray-haired man in a light brown, tall-crown Stetson and western clothing knocked on the door jam at the ranch house. A shorter, younger man dressed similarly, except with a sweat-stained gray low-crowned hat, stood behind him.

Luz McPherson opened the thick plank door of the adobe-walled house and pushed the screen door back.

The man stepped away and snatched the hat from his head. "Afternoon, Miz McPherson."

"Afternoon, Sheriff Russell. What can I do for you?"

"Well, I…uh…Ma'am…I…"

"Get to it, Sheriff."

"Yessum…you see, Ben Wilford's issued a complaint against you fer horse stealin', an'…"

"Horse stealin'?"

"Uh…yessum. Uh, Deputy Henry here went through your herd on the way out here an' found four head with the Circle W brand on 'em."

Luz crossed her arms over her bosom. "Sheriff, mind if I ask the deputy some questions?"

"Uh…shore, Ma'am, go right ahead." He stepped back a little so Luz could address the young man.

"Shorty, how long you known me?"

The deputy cut his eyes at the sheriff. "Ah, since I wuz 'bout fifteen, reckon, when I worked for yuh."

"Uh-huh…an' what kind of stock do I run?"

"Well, only'st top grade breedin' horse flesh, Ma'am."

Luz nodded. "An' those mares in my herd wearin' a Circle W brand…How would you grade them?"

He cut his eyes at the sheriff again. "'Bout medium to low grade, Ma'am…Seen you cull better."

"Right…an' do you really think I'd sully my herd with inferior stock?"

"No, Ma'am, never known you to."

She looked back at Sheriff Russell. "Now, Case, does it stand to reason I would steal horses nowhere near good as my own?"

The sheriff scratched his sweat plastered gray thinning hair. "Well, Luz, put it thataway, reckon not."

"An' how would you suppose they got into my herd?"

He looked down at his dusty boots with the run over heels. "Uh…If'n I wuz a bettin' man, I'd say somebody put 'em there apurpose."

Luz cocked her head. "You don't say?"

"Yessum, guess I do say."

"Now, I suggest you ride on over to Wilford's an' tell him, his little trick ain't gonna work…an' if his mares ain't outta my herd by tomorrow, I'm gonna round 'em up an' drive 'em into town to the sale barn…Tell 'em to send him the check. Scrub mares 'er bringin' 'bout fifty dollars…if they're bred."

Sheriff Russell arched both eyebrows. "He ain't gonna take kindly to that, Miz McPherson."

Luz leaned forward until she almost touched his nose. "I don't care."

PALO DURO CANYON

Loraine's eyes rolled back up in her head as she slumped slowly to the side. Bone quickly sidepassed Hildebrandt, wrapped his thick arm around her tiny waist and pulled her over to his lap. He leaned her back against his muscular chest.

"Bear Dog, bring Sweet Face."

The wolf-dog grabbed one of the reins that had slipped from Loraine's fingers and led the mare after Bone as he walked Hildebrandt along Silke and Haven's tracks. He carried the unconscious Loraine like a child with one arm, his other holding his reins.

Twenty minutes later, they reached the girls and Berkley. They had stopped at the south bank of Tule Creek as it merged with the river to water the horses.

Silke was the first to notice Bone walking Hildebrandt around the bend in the river toward them just before the confluence of the two waterways. She dropped *Lakná's* reins and ran over to meet them.

"What's wrong with Loraine?"

"She got hit…didn't let me know till ya'll left. Passed out while we were talking." He lifted her over to Silke who had been joined by Berkley, Haven, and Elizabeth.

"Didn't stop to check if it's a graze or the bullet's still in there." He dismounted, opened his saddlebags on his side and took out a small black leather kit. "Haven, you want to take Hildebrandt and Sweet Face and get 'em some water?"

"Can do."

Bear Dog had led the mare in right behind Bone.

Haven took the rein from his mouth, grabbed Hildebrandt's and led them over to the clear spring fed Tule Creek.

Bone took Loraine from Silke and Berkley, carried her over to a grassy area near the creek and gently laid her down. "Reg, need a fire and hot water...*pronto*."

Elizabeth squatted down next to her and looked up at Bone. "Is Loraine gonna be alright?"

"I hope so, honey."

Bone knelt down beside his wife, unlaced her doeskin top down the front and peeled it back. He eased the blood-soaked leather from around the wound.

He pulled the camo tee Loraine had worn since they were accidentally transported back to this time she was wearing underneath up to her armpit. Bone took a gauze pad from his kit to clean the blood away.

Reg was quickly building a fire with dry driftwood and some periderm he scraped from the inside of a piece of cottonwood bark for tinder. He took a phosphorus match from a vest pocket and lit the powder dry inner bark.

The yellow flame from the strike-anywhere match slowly ate into the light brown fibrous material, catching it on fire—it quickly spread to the twigs and stems on top. Berkley added some larger branches.

Bone wet another gauze pad with some carbolic acid to clean any fibers from the wound, and then he held the pad against the bleeding wound.

"Silke, hold this for a few minutes. Looks like she was lucky. Bullet glanced off a rib, but I gotta sew that gouge up. Need my needle and thread…Hope she stays out for a few more minutes." He glanced over at Berkley. "How quick on that water?"

"About three minutes."

"Blow on it, need it in two."

"Do my best."

Bone stepped over to the paniers Berkley had removed from Ted before he took him to the water.

He dug a bottle of *Sauza Tequila* out and carried it over to where Loraine lay.

Bone knelt down, put the bottle between his knees, took his needle and a spool of black linen thread from the kit. "Let me check the wound, Silke. Thread that needle for me and I'll sterilize it with some of the tequila."

"It's better than carbolic acid?"

"Twice over." Bone chuckled.

"What is it?"

"Oh, just remembered a demonstration our coach gave us in college about alcohol." He giggled as he peeled the pad away from Loraine's wound. "Stopped bleeding...Good job, Silke."

Elizabeth brought a small pan of steaming water from the fire. "It's ready."

"Thank you, honey...Now, pour some on this pad so I can get all this blood wiped away..." He looked up as Elizabeth did what he asked.

"Anyway, the coach had a glass of water and a glass of tequila on a table. He dropped a worm in the water and we all watched it swim around. Then he took another worm and dropped it in the tequila."

"What happened?" asked Silke.

"Well, that poor worm just shriveled up and died, right there."

"And?" Silke cocked her head.

"I just shrugged and said, 'Well, Coach, guess it means if you drink alcohol…you won't have any worms'…He threw one of the glasses at me."

"Oh, Bone, that's awful."

He looked down at Loraine, who was looking back at him.

"True story, babe…How do you feel?"

"How do you think I feel? Like I've been kicked in the ribs by big Ted over there."

He grinned. "Well, pretty close, darlin'…Wish you'd have stayed out for another minute or so."

She frowned. "Why? So you can tell another one of your terrible jokes?"

"No…I've got to sew you up and it's going to hurt like the dickens."

"Well, give me a couple of hits of that tequila before you start."

He nodded, lifted her head and held the bottle to her lips. She took one swallow, then another, squinched her face and closed one eye.

"Start sewing, but be nice…Give me one more."

She had another drink, then she took a breath.

Bone poured some of the one hundred proof, fifty percent alcohol liquor on the wound. Loraine gritted her teeth, moaned, and arched her back slightly.

Bone looked over at her. "Want a stick to bite on, babe?"

She shook her head. "No…I want your finger."

"Uh, that'll have to wait." He poured some more on the needle and thread. "Ready?"

Loraine took several yoga breaths, relaxed her body, and nodded.

Bone had Silke pour some tequila on his hands. He pinched the skin around Loraine's wound together with his left hand, pushed the needle through and to the other side and nodded to Silke to cut it with the cuticle scissors from his kit.

She snipped the black thread, Bone quickly tied it off and ran the needle through again.

Loraine's only reaction were the muscles in her jaw rippling as she ground her teeth together.

"That should do it." He tied off the seventh stitch.

Loraine blew air out of her mouth. "Thank God, thought I was going to have to hurt you. Felt like you were planting potatoes."

"Waa-waa-waa...You gotta quit getting shot, babe."

"Yeah, I'm one up on you."

Bone wiggled his eyebrows. "For now."

Silke shook her head. "How did ya'll ever figure out you were in love to get married?"

"She held a gun on me."

"Damn you, Bone."

"No, actually, she threw me over her head with some of her Kung Fu stuff, sat on my chest and we both had an epiphany at the same time. Got married the next week."

Loraine smiled. "Your little brother said we would back four years ago."

Haven looked at Bone. "You got a little brother?"

"Well, he's younger, but bigger by a couple of inches an' about thirty pounds...Family calls him Tiny or T-bone...He wanted to be best man, but we couldn't get that worked out...He's a Texas Ranger."

Silke nodded. "Like to meet him sometime."

Haven added, "Me too."

Bone grinned and shrugged. "Who knows...could happen."

Silke smiled. "With you two, anything can happen…Guess we just as well settle in for the evenin'. Don't think Loraine is gonna feel like ridin' for a bit."

§§§

CHAPTER THIRTEEN

BLUE WATER, TEXAS

Mad Jack Ketcher and his men, Luke Brown, J.D. Burdick, and Ace Cole reined up in front of Murphy's Wet Goods, the only saloon in the small cow town.

They let their horses drink their fill at the wooden water trough, then dismounted, led them to the hitching rails, loosened their girths, and tied them off.

There were several horses of varying colors already standing hipshot at the other rails.

The four men removed their hats and used them to slap the dust from their trousers and shirt sleeves, then set them back on their heads and pushed through the batwing doors.

They stood just inside as their eyes adjusted to the dim light of the twenty-five by fifty foot room that stank of cigarette smoke, stale beer, and urine.

A skinny man in a black derby, a sort of white shirt with black arm garters, was banging *Buffalo Gals* on a rinky-tink piano against the back wall.

Several men at nearby tables were attempting to sing along with the out-of-tune piano.

Other tables had men playing poker or blackjack.

Two rather heavy girls-of-the-line in low cut saloon dresses—showing an inordinate amount of cleavage that could literally pass for the cheeks of their ample butts—worked the room.

The men sauntered to the twenty-four inch wide plank bar that was set on empty whiskey barrels placed every six feet.

A large potbellied bartender, wearing a once-white apron around his prodigious girth, walked down from the other end of the bar with a dirty towel over his shoulder. “What’ll it be, gents? I’m Murphy.”

Mad Jack glanced at the others, then back. “Got’ny cold beer?”

“Well, depends on what you mean by cold…it ain’t hot…that what you mean? Take it or leave it.”

“We’ll take it. Need to wash some of this trail dust from our throats.”

“You got it. Be a nickel a glass…twenty cents.”

Kercher pitched a quarter on the planks. “Close enough.”

J.D. turned around and leaned back against the bar. “Don’t look like the place is jumpin’.”

Luke glanced over his shoulder. “Meby it’s early yet…ain’t quite sundown.”

Burdick turned back around. “Yeah, could be.”

Ace unscrewed the lid to a gallon jug sitting on the bar, fished out a couple of pickled banty hen eggs with the tongs and popped them in his mouth. He chewed a couple of times, swallowed and almost gagged.

"Good God amighty them things is awful." He looked up at the bartender as he set their beer mugs on the planks. "What'd you pickle those things with, horse piss?"

He grinned. "How'd you guess. That's another dime."

"Do I pay you or you pay me?"

"Like it better the first way. Got some purty good beef stew back in the kitchen…ya'll want some."

Ace squinted his eyes. "Ain't like them eggs, air they?"

"Naw, we use local beef. Ranchers find a dead cow on their place, they drag it into town…I cut it up. Good aged steaks, too."

Ace shook his head. "Believe I'll pass."

The bartender grabbed his big belly and roared with laughter. "Haw! Had you goin' didn't I?"

"Mean you wuz funnin' me?"

"Shore…Don't have much entertainment 'round here…gotta make my own. My sweet wife's cookin' will make you slap yo mama…trust me on that."

"What 'bout them eggs?" Ace pointed at the jug.

"Oh, buy them from a drummer…Comes through here ever six months er so."

Ace nodded. "What I figured."

The bartender glanced at the four men. "Ya'll want some of that stew?"

Mad Jack nodded. "I'll try a bowl…Ain't no good, I'll jest shootyuh."

The bartender laughed again and nodded. "Heard that afore, too." He turned and headed into the kitchen through a door behind the bar.

J.D. turned to Jack. "Boss, 'stead of waitin' here in this jerkwater town, why don't we head east an' jest meet up with those folks?"

Kercher looked at the other man. "Damn, Burdick, you do use yer head fer somethin' 'sides a hat rack…Purty good idee. Don't see no place to get a room anyhoo."

PALO DURO CANYON

Loraine was leaning propped on her saddle with a blanket up to her waist. She was wearing a spare white tee they had gotten from her saddlebags.

Bear Dog was stretched out beside her.

Haven walked back up from the creek with her wet camo tee and her doeskin top. "Got most of the blood out, Loraine. Cold water an' some of your lilac lye soap did the trick. Can stitch up the holes when they dry…I'll hang 'em on this big limb stickin' out from that red oak. Be dry by mornin', I 'spect."

"Thank you, Haven. Did anybody go back an get my magazine?"

Bone reached in his parfleche bag and pulled the four inch long black metal magazine out and held it up. "This what you were talkin' about, babe?"

Loraine wrinkled her brow. "When did you go back…"

"You took a little nap after I stitched you up…probably from all that tequila you drank."

"Damn you, Bone, I only had three."

"Yeah, but you only weigh a hundred an ten pounds…don't take much."

Loraine nodded. "Point…I'm gettin' hungry, anybody start supper?" She started to sit up, but stopped with a stab of pain, laid back down, and groaned. "Oh, my that's sore."

Silke looked up from over at the campfire. "Funny you should ask…Just happen to be fryin' up some fish we caught while Bone was gone lookin' for your magazine…Got fried catfish, hot water cornbread an' pickled peaches."

"Oh, yum." Loraine glanced at Bone and crooked her finger at him.

He stepped over and squatted down beside her. "What, babe?"

"Any chance of doing the Lucy thing on my side…kinda speed up the healing?"

He glanced over at Berkley having a cup of coffee on the other side of the camp and frowned. "Need to send our companion on a little errand or something. Don't particularly want to get into the time travel or the visiting alien with him…Something about him I don't trust. Can't put my finger on it."

Loraine nodded. "Yeah, Bear Dog doesn't like him either…always trust a dog's instincts."

Bone nodded. "Especially his…One of the smartest animals I've ever been around…Knows what you're thinking before you do."

Darkness had fallen after they had eaten and cleaned up the utensils and the millions upon millions points of light were twinkling into view from east to west across the blackness of the sky.

One of the brightest stars in the void to be visible was Venus, just above the western horizon.

Elizabeth pointed to it as it grew into view when the sun settled below the horizon. "What's that star, Silke?"

"That's a planet, honey…named Venus. Known as the evening star…Look to the left and up a bit…see that red one?"

"Uh-huh."

"That's another planet, Mars."

"Golly…Are there people there?"

Silke shrugged. "We don't know."

"Are there people anywhere out there?"

Silke glanced at Bone.

He nodded. "Could be, honey. There was an article in the Dallas newspaper on April 19, 1898, reporting that a spacecraft crashed at Aurora, Texas, on April 17…It said the pilot 'was not of this world'…They buried him in the local cemetery there."

Elizabeth cocked her head. "What's a spacecraft?"

Loraine lifted her head a little. "It's a type of ship that travels through all those stars up there, like we have ships that sail all over our mighty oceans."

"I think all that's hokum," said Berkley as he pitched the dregs of his after dinner coffee into the fire where it sizzled and popped on a burning piece of driftwood.

Bone glanced over at him. "Well, maybe not. I've been to that cemetery and there is a fresh grave there with a red sandstone marker…Had a triangle ship carved into it and said, 'Not of this World' on the inscription…And, as I'm sure you know, there is nothing in this little speck in the cosmos world of ours that can fly, except for birds…There was a lot of debris there that people were hauling off for souvenirs."

Haven joined in, "My mother told me…she was a school teacher, you know…that the Sumerians, of ancient Babylonia, called their gods the *Anunnaki* which meant, 'They from the stars who came.' and that was over 5,000 years ago."

Silke got up and refilled her cup from the pot next to the fire. "Personally, I think it's the height of narcissism to think of all the millions of stars out there, that are suns just like ours, that there wouldn't be other planets…like Earth, too."

Elizabeth frowned. "What's 'nar-ci-si-sm?"

Silke chuckled. "It's an arrogant sense of self-importance, Lizbeth…Like someone thinkin' they're the only fish in the big wide ocean.…It originated from Greek mythology, where the young Narcissus fell in love with his own image reflected in a pool of water."

"Oh, how dumb."

Bone grinned and nodded. "Now you have it, Lizabeth."

Berkley grunted, got to his feet and walked down to the creek. "I'm going for a little walk."

He walked off into the darkness as the frogs in the creek momentarily stopped their croaking as he passed. The night birds and crickets soon also resumed their songs as the fish in the creek continued to pop the surface after insects landing on the water.

Across the creek on one of the many mesas, a pack of coyotes began to tune up with their night serenade to the gibbous moon that was just rising in the east.

Bone and Loraine exchanged glances. He looked at Haven. "Keep watch and let me know when you hear him coming back."

She frowned. "How will I know? It's dark."

"The frogs, birds, and crickets up close will stop again."

Haven nodded. "Right."

§§§

CHAPTER FOURTEEN

BLUE WATER, TEXAS

The gibbous moon was about twenty degrees above the eastern horizon as Mad Jack and his gang trotted their mounts east.

They pulled rein at the southwest bank of *Tierra Blanco* Creek, a little over five miles east of Blue Water.

Jack stepped down from his gelding. "Just as well camp here, fellers. This'll be the last water till we git to the Palo Duro. Make sure the boys drink plenty 'fore we leave of the mornin'."

Ace Cole looked at the slow moving clear water creek, then at Mad Jack. "Don't this creek run into the Prairie Dog Town Fork of the Red in the Palo Duro? Why don't we jest foller it?"

"Because, numb-nuts, it winds all over hell an' half of Georgia up purt near back to Amarillo 'fore it gits to the Palo Duro. Now does that answer yer final question?"

Ace took off his hat and wiped the inside of the sweat band with his blue wild rag. "Oh, yeah…Reckon that's so. Lot's shorter cuttin' 'cross."

Jack shook his head. "Yuh think?"

The high-pitched screech of a west Texas blue quail sounded in the darkness.

Luke turned his head. "Listen, be a covey of blue quail cross the creek. Too bad it ain't light enough to see 'em."

"What's the difference 'tween a blue quail an' a bobwhite?" J.D. looked at Luke as he pulled the tack from his grulla.

"Damn'f I know."

Mad Jack shook his head. "Don't ya'll know nothin?...Blue quails is kindly blue an' got a crest of feathers on the top of their heads an' bobwhites are brown with white stripes 'cross their faces."

He dumped his tack near a ring of rocks some other traveler had built previously. "Bobwhites make that three whistle call an' will fly up when disturbed...Blues will jest screech like that one an' run on the ground through the brush...Lots harder to hit than a bobwhite."

"How do you know all that stuff, Jack?" asked Luke.

"It's why I'm the boss an' ya'll're not...Now git a fire built while yer restin'...Needin' some coffee...Then supper."

PALO DURO CANYON

Bone knelt down beside Loraine, reached across her body and placed both hands, one on top of the other, gently, over her bandaged wound.

Bear Dog sat up watching him, his head was cocked.

Haven stood down near the creek, keeping her ears open and her eyes peeled for Berkley coming back along the creek bank.

The pale moonlight reflected and scintillated like thousands of golden diamonds from the tiny ripples across the surface.

Silke sat next to Bear Dog with her knees pulled up to her chest and both arms wrapped around them.

Bone took several deep cleansing breaths and dropped his chin to his chest.

Nothing happened for a few moments, then finally a soft blue glow seemed to emanate from his hands. The light slowly grew brighter and brighter until it encompassed both him and Loraine.

His breathing was slow and appeared almost nonexistent as in a deep meditative state. The ethereal glow intensified a little more, and then began to fade away like wispy smoke or fog on a windless night.

Silke moved quickly to catch Bone to keep him from falling on top of Loraine as he slowly toppled over. She pulled him to the side, catching his head from hitting the ground, when he collapsed like an accordion folding up.

Loraine's brown eyes flickered several times before they opened. She first looked around as if she were confused before her gaze settled on Bone's massive body lying crumpled beside her.

Her bosom rose several times as she took several breaths, then she looked up at Silke and mouthed the word, *water*.

Silke was prepared as she had seen Bone do the same thing to her baby brother when Padrino pulled him from the cold water of the well back at their homeplace—she had a canteen beside her. Silke removed the stopper and handed it to Loraine.

Bear Dog crawled forward on his belly and licked Bone on the side of the face several times.

The big man moaned slightly, pushed his face away and mumbled, "Not now, honey." His gold-flecked eyes snapped open staring directly into Bear Dog's blue ones.

He shook his head, sat up and rubbed between the wolf-dog's ears. "Thanks, buddy, but I need some water."

Elizabeth brought him another canteen as Loraine was drinking from Silke's again.

"Here, Bone, Silke told me you would need this…That was amazin' what you did. How did you do it?"

Silke leaned over and took the almost empty canteen from Loraine. "The Bible calls it, 'the laying on of hands', Lizbeth…Bone shared some of his life energy with Loraine to help her heal."

Bone turned the canteen up and almost drained it. "Ahh, that was good…Needed that." He looked over at Loraine. "How do you feel, babe?"

She felt of her side, took a deep breath, and smiled. "Much better. Still a touch sore, but nothing like it was before." Loraine lifted the bandage up. "Almost healed closed…Have to take out the stitches tomorrow."

"Well, sharpen your acting chops around Berkley for the next day or so."

"Can do, the memory's still fresh. Don't think I'd ever want to be a method actor though."

"What's that, Loraine?…Method actor?" Elizabeth was confused.

"Oh, it's a rather self-indulging, arrogant acting style where the actor tries to actually experience a feeling or emotion instead of just using their imagination."

Elizabeth shook her head as she furrowed her brow. "I don't understand."

"That's all right, honey, most actors don't either."

Haven walked back into camp from down at the creek. "Frogs an' birds have stopped." She looked at Bone. "Just what was that you did?"

"Good girl…Tell you later." Bone got to his feet, a little shakily at first, but quickly stabilized, grabbed his blue graniteware cup, stepped over to the fire and poured himself some coffee using one of his deerskin gloves for a hot-pad.

"Thought I saw a strange blue glow through the trees from up the creek a ways. Did ya'll see it?"

"Huh?…No, I didn't." Bone looked at Berkley as he stepped from the darkness into the firelight—then at the girls. "Ya'll see anything?"

They all shook their heads.

"Maybe it was the ghosts or spirits of all those horses the army slaughtered fightin' the Comanche, Bodie was tellin' us about." Silke had a slight wry grin on her face. "Or maybe an alien from the stars."

Berkley lifted a single eyebrow and frowned. "Yes, of course."

Bone cleared his throat. "Think we should post a lookout for tonight. Don't know if that was all the renegades or not…The bodies were gone when I went back looking for Loraine's magazine."

"Good idea, Bone, I'll take first watch."

Haven glanced at her cousin. "I'll relieve you at midnight, Silke."

Berkley nodded. "I'll take over then at three, Haven."

"And I'll finish it off to dawn and start the morning fire," said Bone.

Bear Dog woofed.

Silke rubbed his broad head. "Don't really think we have anything to worry about with Bear Dog on the watch. I can assure you that no one…or thing, is going to come close to camp without him knowin' 'bout it."

Bone nodded. "The horses and Ted will do a good job, too…Fiona told me her paint mule, Spot, was good as any watchdog…Said saved her bacon several times. Our guys're upwind and long as it doesn't switch, they'll know if anybody's coming from that direction…'specially Lizbeth's Calico. He's a mustang."

Silke looked up at the clouds scudding across the starlit sky and temporarily covering the half-moon. "May storm tomorrow. Got clouds moving in from the northwest.

Bone nodded. "It's springtime. Going to get passing thunder-bumpers. Whoever's on watch needs to keep an eye on the clouds, too…Don't want to get caught this close to the creek in a downpour."

Silke looked back off to the northwest. "I would bet we hear thunder or at least see some lightning off that way…first." She pointed. "Not hot enough for heat lightning, yet."

Bone's grin spread across his face as he sniffed the air. "Going to get rain in any case by tomorrow…Can already smell it.…Oh! Just a thought. Don't look at the fire while you're on guard."

Haven raised her eyebrows. "Why?"

"Ruins your night vision. Can't see squat for ten to fifteen minutes after looking at flames."

"Ooh, makes sense."

"I'll go check the hobbles on the horses and Ted first." Silke glanced at Bone. "There still plenty coffee left?"

"Is now, but suspect you'll have to make another pot before your shift is over."

"I'll go ahead an' make one now for ya'll, 'fore I crawl in my blankets."

Silked hugged the little girl. "Well, thank you, Lizbeth, that's very nice."

"I just want to help."

"I know you do, honey. I know you do."

No one noticed Berkley studying the panniers stacked over beside the saddles and other truck…

§§§

CHAPTER FIFTEEN

PALO DURO CANYON

Silke made one more turn down to the creek and over to the area where the stock was hobbled. Bear Dog padded alongside her.

All was well, the night creatures continued their music, except for the coyotes. They had not performed their serenade for several hours—not unusual for the feral canines once they started their hunt.

She put another log on the fire, stepped over to Haven's bedroll and gently shook her shoulder. "Wake up, cuz. Your turn."

Haven looked up at Silke's face and blinked several times. "Huh? What?...Right...Sleepin' hard." She sat up.

"Added some wood to the fire...coffee's hot."

The sable-haired beauty rubbed the sleep from her eyes and reached over for her calf-high boots. She shook them upside down to dislodge any possible borders, pulled them on her feet and stood up.

"Good, need some...Hear any thunder yet?"

Silky shook her head. "Not yet."

Haven glanced around. "Where's Bear Dog?"

"Do what? Oh...He was here a few minutes ago. Guess he's out doin' his thing or out with Ted. He'll be back, directly, I would imagine."

Haven strapped on her gunbelt and slipped on her sheepskin jacket against the nighttime chill. "Now for some of that coffee...Go ahead an' turn in, cuz, I'm good."

"See you in the mornin'." Silke headed to her bedroll which she had already laid out.

Haven poured herself a cup of the steaming Arbuckles' brew. She rolled the warm graniteware cup back and forth between her hands, blew across the surface and took a sip. "Mmm, good."

She looked off to the northwest and saw the first flicker of lightning well beyond the horizon. "Yep, comin'."

The half-moon had traversed across the sky until it was at the one o'clock position with more and more clouds moving across its face, periodically obscuring the limited light.

Haven strolled down to the rippling creek, listening to the soothing sounds of the night, including the bass slapping the surface with their tails. She looked up at the part of the milky strip resembling a thin smoke plume that ran across the sky known as the Milky Way and shook her head.

"Amazin', simply amazin,"

She recalled what Silke had said about the stars or suns all probably having planets, like Earth, circling around them and what appeared as a cloud stretching across the heavens like a wide river was actually uncountable stars—like grains of sand on a beach.

Haven turned to look at the hobbled animals in their graze and noticed their ears had perked up—they were all looking to the north. She held her cup in her left hand, always keeping her right free and near the butt of her Peacemaker as Silke had instructed her. Haven slipped the hammer thong free.

Ted blew loudly through his nostrils and was followed by Elizabeth's mustang, Calico, doing the same—a sign of apprehension or displeasure with equines.

She pitched the remains of her coffee on the bank at her feet, loosened her .38-40 in its holster, and stepped over to stand in the blackness beside a large cottonwood.

Ted stamped a front hoof twice—another sign of nervousness.

The night sounds ceased. The quietness was abruptly shattered by a high-pitched scream mixed with snarls and the sounds of brush being disturbed. The horses and mule bunched up, all facing the noise, ready to defend themselves since they couldn't run.

The screams and growls stopped, but the noise of the brush being rustled didn't. Haven heard what sounded like someone running through the leaves and branches.

Everyone in the camp was on their feet, guns in hand. Silke had moved next to Elizabeth and crouched between her and the north side of the camp.

Bear Dog trotted into the firelight and sat down. He looked around at everyone as if to say, *What are ya'll doin' up*? There was a trace of blood glistening around his black muzzle.

"Well, looks like we had a visitor Bear Dog didn't like much. Bet it was a renegade slipping up trying to steal a horse or two…Indians love to do that at night, call it 'counting coup'." Bone grinned as he looked down at the hybrid coal black canine looking back up at him and wagging his tail. "Gonna break 'em from suckin' eggs, aren't you boy?"

Bear Dog *woo-wooed* his response, spun around twice, sat back down and cocked his head.

Berkley stepped over to the fire with his cup and filled it. "Well, Haven, I'm up. Not that long to my shift…Just as well go ahead and start it now…If that's all right?"

"Fine with me, Reg." She glanced at Silke, who nodded. "Did see some flashes way over the horizon. Storm could be headed our way.

He nodded. "Keep my eyes open."

Everyone moseyed back to their sleeping tarps and turned back in.

Berkley took a sip of his coffee and watched them roll up in their blankets.

Thirty minutes later Berkley could plainly hear Bone's even snoring. Everyone else seemed to be deep in slumber, too. He pitched the dregs of his coffee out, set his cup on a rock, eased over to the panniers and saddlebags, and squatted down.

Berkley opened the top of one of the panniers and felt around inside. He grimaced, removed his hand and proceeded to do the same with the other—what he was looking for wasn't there.

Reg picked up what he thought was Silke's saddlebags and started unbuckling one side. Before he could finish with the first buckle, he was interrupted by a low guttural growl to his right.

Bear Dog's nose was less than four inches from his face. His black lips were curled back in a snarl—a drop of saliva, glistening from the flickering fire, dripped from one of his inch long fangs. It was the same look Bear Dog had when he 'smiled'—but his tail wasn't wagging.

Berkley froze. Only his blue-gray eyes cut to Bear Dog's teeth. Without moving his head or eyes, he slowly pulled his hand from the buckle and eased the bags back next to the panniers. He cautiously rose to his feet and stepped backward—first one foot, then another. Bear Dog didn't move, but his blue eyes followed every move.

Berkley took one step at a time backward to the rock where he had set his cup and softly exhaled as Bear Dog laid down beside the saddlebags, placing his muzzle on top of his paws—his expressionless eyes never leaving him.

His shaking hands picked up the cup and he cautiously worked his way over to the fire to fill it from the pot. He took a deep breath, exhaled again and glanced off to the north.

There were flashes of light over the horizon, but much more often than earlier. The light show resembled an artillery battle in a war—but no sound, as yet, reached his ears.

"Uh-oh."

The horses and Ted nervously chuffed and snorted as they sensed the coming storm.

Berkley sauntered over to Bone's bedroll and nudged the big man's shoulder.

Bone's Marine Corps training kicked in and he was instantly awake, his hand gripping his Smith & Wesson 500, which had been by his side. His gold-flecked eyes focused on Berkley.

"What?"

"Getting an increasingly good light show off to the northwest…I would recommend we seek higher ground."

Bone sat up and shifted his gaze to the northwest horizon and noted the increasing flashes as they appeared to be moving closer.

"Think you're right." He threw his blanket back, shook out his Apache moccasins, pulled them on and laced them up the side. "Add some more wood to the fire, we'll have some coffee before we pack up."

Berkley nodded as Bone patted Loraine's shapely rump under her blanket laid out next to his. "Wake up, Babe, we gotta move."

She blinked several times and looked up at him. "What?"

"Storm coming. How do you feel?"

"A little sore, but all right."

He leaned over close to her ear. "Don't forget to play along…be gimpy."

"I know…Check and see if my top and tee are dry."

"Yessum."

Bone stepped over to the limb where Haven had hung Loraine's doeskin top and tee shirt and felt of them. Satisfied, he pulled them free and carried them back over to his wife's bedroll.

"Here you go, Babe. Dry enough."

She nodded and slipped the soft leather top back on and laced it up. "Thank you, dear."

TIERRA BLANCO CREEK

Luke stood over the slumbering Mad Jack Ketcher. "Boss…Boss…Need to wake up."

Ketcher blinked and looked up at his underling. "This better be good, Brown."

"Uh…Got a storm comin', Boss." He pointed at the dark line of clouds repeatedly being illuminated by cloud to cloud and cloud to ground lightning just above the horizon.

Mad Jack rolled over and looked the direction Luke was pointing. "Umm…Got a point. Need to git away from this creek." He looked at a post oak close to his bedroll and saw a high water mark four feet up the trunk. "In a bad spot. Git the others up. Let's get the hell outta here."

"Right, Boss…Hey! Everbody! Gotta load up an' git to high ground. Storm comin'."

PALO DURO CANYON

Bone threw another half-hitch on the panniers hanging on both sides of Ted's pack tree. The big Tennessee mule looked back at him. Bone finished and rubbed him between his eyes.

"Sorry, big guy, hate to disturb your rest, but need to find some shelter."

The mule grunted at him.

"Glad you approve."

He moved to Hildebrandt, laid the horsehair filled saddlepad over his back and slung his square skirted Texas, double rigged saddle on top. He pulled a bubble up under the gullet so the saddle wouldn't pinch his whithers and cinched up the front, and then the back girth.

Bone stepped over, did the same to Loraine's Sweet Face and led her over to her mistress. "Here you go, Babe."

She handed him her soogan to tie behind her cantle. He helped her mount with a little panache for Berkley's benefit.

He finished tying his soogan and saddlebags on Hildebrandt and mounted. Bone and Loraine walked their horses over to where Silke, Elizabeth, and Haven were waiting.

Berkley joined them with Ted in tow and glanced at Loraine. "You seem to be doing much better, Loraine."

She nodded as she leaned over in her saddle like she was taking some pressure off her side. "Yes, sore as a risin', but it beats the alternative."

"I suppose that's true."

Silke glanced at Bone. "Where to, oh, great and exalted leader?"

"Up creek to what the map calls the Rock Garden. Should find some cover there."

His sentence was punctuated by a flash of lightning followed a few seconds later by a long rolling peal of thunder that seemed to shake the very ground.

Haven glanced up at the churning clouds, illuminated by the flashing lightning, rapidly approaching them that would cover the half-moon in less than two hours. "Sounds like God's movin' his furniture around."

Loraine side-passed over next to Bone. "I suggest we move with all haste, then, Honey."

§§§

CHAPTER SIXTEEN

PALO DURO CANYON

Bone led the group single file along the narrow trail that ran alongside the river as the eastern horizon, still beyond the storm front, turned pink. Elizabeth was behind him with Loraine and Berkley in back of her.

Bear Dog had taken over Ted's lead rope in his mouth and came next. Haven followed them and Silke brought up the rear.

Lightning came in nonstop cracks and flashes. The smell of ozone permeated the air. Thunder rolled and rumbled continuously.

The heavens opened up and the rain began to fall, first in single dime-sized drops—creating craters in the dust of the trail—that morphed into a veritable downpour, quickly turning the dust to slippery mud.

The water level of the river rose precipitously. Large pieces of flotsam, limbs, and even dead trees washed from the banks, tumbled along in the churning, frothing, muddy water coming from upstream.

The rain came down in sheets, sometimes blowing sideways, making it almost impossible to see.

Bone turned in his saddle and shouted, "Keep up tight. Think I see a cave up ahead."

A scream pierced through the driving rain and thunder as the back hooves of Haven's red roan slipped off the trail and the horse slid sideways and backward down toward the raging tumult below.

SILKE'S RIDE

The game gelding scrambled to maintain some footing, but the ground was too slick. The horse squealed in terror as he slid toward the roaring water…

LLANO ESTACADO

Mad Jack, head down, his hat sucked low on his face to help block the rain, led the others toward a grove of cedar trees almost a mile from the creek.

Each had donned yellow oilcloth slickers against the driving rain—collars turned up.

Visibility was down to less than a hundred feet. It was pure luck the copse of cedars was directly in front of them. The trees wouldn't offer shelter from the rain, but would give a modicum of protection from the gusting wind.

They stopped inside the grove, turning their horse's rumps to the wind and hunkered down to weather the storm.

The squall line was up to fifty miles wide and moved southeast at thirty-five to forty miles an hour. The fierce spring storm was dumping over four inches an hour of rain—streams, creeks, and rivers would all be over their banks in short order.

"Damn good thang we got away from that creek when we did," screamed Ace.

Jack squinted his eyes at the man through the water running off his hat brim. "Brilliant statement, there, Ace."

Cole cast a glare back at Mad Jack. "Glad you think so, Kercher."

PALO DURO CANYON

Silke untied her braided rawhide *riata* from the right side of her saddle, quickly built a loop and swinging it only once, let it fly. It dropped cleanly over *d'Artagnan's* head to settle around his muscular neck.

Silke dallied off on her wet saddlehorn and kicked *Lakná* in the ribs, even though it wasn't necessary. The big dun mustang knew what to do—he turned to the right and dug into the soft earth until he grabbed purchase.

The rope slipped on the wet leather of the saddlehorn and after Silke flipped two more dallies—it stopped.

Bone had gotten turned around in the trail and slung a loop of his own over the gallant roan's neck as the horse's rear end was almost in the raging river.

The giant half-Friesian's massive, added, strength took effect as he and Silke's gelding pulled Haven and *d'Artagnan* back up on the trail and away from sure death.

Bone walked Hildebrandt over where he could remove both his and Silke's ropes from the roan's neck. "You all right, Haven?"

She nodded, even though her eyes were still big as saucers.

Bone smiled at her. "Stay tight, now." He turned Hildebrandt back around and led the group up toward a cave with a very high, though fairly narrow, opening.

Haven nodded again.

He turned once he was inside and moved over, waving everyone on into the cave. "Work on to the back…It's dry back there.

Loraine rode up beside Elizabeth. “All right, honey?”

She nodded. “Wet is all…Calico did good.” She patted the paint on his neck.

“Yes, he did.” Loraine smiled at her.

Bear Dog trotted in behind Berkley, calmly leading Ted.

“Ya’ll see any wood back there?” Bone stepped down from the saddle and started loosening Hildebrandt’s latigo.

Silke also dismounted. “There’s some, Bone. Looks like someone else has taken refuge in here at one time or another…Fire pit, too…Get started on one soon’s I pull this wet tack and try to rubdown *Lakná* with one of my spare undershirts.”

Bone jerked his truck from Hildebrandt, then unsaddled Elizabeth’s mustang, laying the wet saddle blankets on top of the saddles, before stepping over to tend to Loraine’s mare.

Elizabeth hugged Bone’s waist. “Thank you, Bone. I’ll help Silke with the fire.”

“Well, that’s real nice, Lizbeth…Sure she’ll appreciate that.” He patted her back.

Haven finished untacking *d'Artagnan* and wiping him down. She turned and moved over to

Bone, reached up, threw her arms around his neck, buried her face against his thick chest, and burst into tears.

She caught her breath and looked up, her eyes full. “Tha…thank you, Bone…Thought we were goin’ to drag Silke an’ *Lakná* in…in there with us…Don’t know when I’ve been so scared.”

Bone hugged her tightly. “I know, Haven, I know…Glad I was there. No way ya’ll were goin’ to pull Hildebrandt in, no way.” He gave her an extra squeeze. “Now go help with Ted and see if you can scout up some more wood back in there…Don’t want to catch a chill.”

She smiled, raised up on her tip toes, kissed his cheek, turned and headed back toward Ted and Bear Dog.

Berkley finally got the wet slipknots free and undid the half-hitches to free the panniers. He set one on the ground, walked around to the other side and pulled the other one off.

Bear Dog sat in front of the big mule watching Berkley tend to his friend.

Haven walked up, dug a croker sack from one of the panniers and commenced to give Ted a rubdown to get much of the water off. The big mule shook, helping shake some of it free.

Bear Dog followed suit to Ted's actions and shook, too, then he trotted over to the side of the cave. He turned around several times and scratched the sand to make himself a hole to lie down in.

After scratching in several directions, he turned around several more times and curled up in the depression.

Haven stepped over after drying Ted as best she could with the tow sack and rubbed it down Bear Dog's still damp fur.

His top lip curled up in his smile, like a snarl, but his tail pounded the ground behind him in pleasure.

She glanced at his tail slapping the dirt, because of the strange sound it made. "That's not right."

Haven scooted over, held Bear Dog's tail in one hand and brushed the sand underneath it away to reveal a dark old wooden surface with a rusted one inch strap of iron running across it. "What's this?" she muttered.

Haven turned her head around. "Bone…Take a look at this."

He made one more swipe with the piece of burlap he was using on Hildebrandt, and stepped over to Haven. "Whatcha got, kiddo?"

"Look here." She pointed at the wood surface she had exposed. "Heard Bear Dog's tail thumping on it."

The wolf-dog had gotten out of his hole, turned around and watched what Haven was doing to his spot with his head cocked.

Bone knelt down as Loraine also stepped over. She was joined by Berkley, Silke, and Elizabeth, all peering at him clearing the rest of the sand away.

His big hands made short work of the loose cave soil around the item. "Box of some sort." He dug down on both sides, grabbed the chest and lifted. "Dang! Heavy…'bout fifty pounds."

Bone pulled the box from the ground with a grunt and set it heavily next to Bear Dog's depression. "Well, children, that's been there a while."

The chest was made of an oiled oak, banded with two rusty iron straps with a rusted lock on the side through a hammered hasp.

Elizabeth pointed into the hole at something white showing from the flickering fire Silke had built.

Bone brushed some more of the dirt away. "A skull!" He cleaned enough of the soil away to lift it free. "Big hole in the front, crushed in…Looks like some kind of hatchet or stone tomahawk, I'd say…Indian."

Loraine nodded. "Believe you're right, Bone…and a direct hit, too."

Bone stuck two of his fingers in the hole, turned and looked around at the others. "You know, I read about a legend of some early pioneers in early 1700s traveling to the Colorado territory attacked by Apaches and wiped out."

"I thought this was Comanche an' Kiowa country?" questioned Silke.

Bone nodded. "Was…after they ran the Apaches off to Arizona in 1724…They had horses the Spaniards left a hundred and fifty years earlier that were running wild across the plains…the Apache were still afoot…Well, the legend goes the pioneers had a box of gold coins they were going to use when they got where ever they were going to set up a settlement…They disappeared…along with their gold."

Berkley raised an eyebrow and pursed his lips as everyone exchanged looks…

§§§

CHAPTER SEVENTEEN

PALO DURO CANYON

"An arrowhead!" Haven held up a black shiny point a little over an inch long with side notches.

Berkley stepped over. "May I see that?" He held out his hand took the arrowhead and held it up to the light from the fire. "Obsidian…Most likely from New Mexico."

Bone looked at the point and nodded. "The Apache hunted from Texas to Arizona...until the Comanche and Kiowa took over Texas, that is."

Berkley handed it back to Haven. "Confirms your earlier hypothesis legend of the Apache attacking the settlers, Bone...Lots of obsidian in New Mexico."

"Uh-huh, I'd say."

Elizabeth wrinkled her brow. "What's obsidian?"

Berkley knelt down to her eye level. "It's volcanic glass, Lizbeth. When a volcano erupts, like they did a long time ago in New Mexico, the black molten glass would flow out from deep in the earth and harden when it reached the surface."

Silke turned to him. "Are you a geologist?"

He shook his head. "Well, no and yes. As I mentioned on the train, I'm a mining engineer and, as such, had to study geology."

"Makes sense." Loraine turned to Bone. "How do we get the box open to see what's inside?"

He shrugged his wide shoulders. "Guess we'll have to take a rock and see if we can break the lock open."

"Have a better suggestion."

Bone looked at Berkley. "And that would be?"

"I'll get my hammer."

"You carry a hammer around with you?" asked Haven.

He grinned. "It's actually called a 'rock pick'. I use it when I'm scouting ridges for minerals and such…Let me get it."

Reg stepped over to his saddlebags, opened one side and pulled out a steel hammer with a leather wrapped handle. It had a square flat-faced head on one end and a sharp point or pick on the other.

He held it up. "*Voilà*."

Elizabeth looked up at Silke. "What's 'wallah' mean?"

"It's a French word that's spelled, *Voilà,* but pronounced, 'wallah', and means basically, 'here it is'…honey."

"Why didn't he just say that?"

Silke shrugged. "I suppose it's easier to say *Voilà*, than 'here it is'. It's kinda like the word victuals, v-i-c-t-u-a-l-s, but pronounced *vittles*…meaning food."

Elizabeth frowned. "Why do they have to spell *vittle*s, v-i-c-t-u-a-l-s?…Who comes up with all this stuff? I think it's dumb."

Berkley smiled at her. "I think you're right, Lizbeth."

The light from the mouth of the cave was increasing as the sun rose above the cloud cover.

Silke looked outside. "Sun's comin' up…Rain's slackin' off."

"Rivers and creeks will run high for a while yet." Bone turned the box so the lock side was facing the fire and looked at Berkley. "Your hammer…Go for it."

"Why don't we just shoot it off?" asked Haven.

Bone chuckled. "Two reasons, missy…one, shooting a gun inside this cave would deafen everyone and scare the bejebers out of the horses and Ted…second reason is that wouldn't be bright because the bullet is soft lead and, even though it's rusted, the lock is steel. The bullet will either splatter or ricochet, and only God knows where…Follow?"

"Oh…see what you mean."

Bone nodded to Berkley.

He knelt down in front of the box and struck the lock sharply with the hammer end of his rock pick—nothing. Berkley hit it again. This time the left side of the lock broke open. He tapped it several more times, opening it further to break some of the rust loose.

Bone reached forward and unhooked the open lock from the hasp and lifted the tang up with a screech. He looked over at Haven.

“All right, girl, you found it…you open it.”

She stepped over and dropped to both knees in front of the box. “Oh, my, my.”

Haven grabbed both sides of the lid, and with some effort because of the rusted hinges, slowly lifted the wooden lid up—she gasped and brought both hands to cover her mouth.

Silke moved closer. “What is it, Haven?”

She looked up and could only point.

Bear Dog stuck his nose over into the box.

The chest was filled almost to the top with gold coins.

Bone glanced at Loraine. “Pard, didn’t you used to collect coins?…What do you call ‘em, a numitist?”

“Actually it’s numismatist, but close enough, Bone.” She reached in and picked up one of the coins. “Oh, wow…1691 French Royal quadruple Louis XIV gold coin…around 28 grams or one ounce.”

"About twenty dollars each, just on the price of gold presently," offered Berkley.

Bone picked up a couple of the coins. "Bet those pilgrims were coming up from New Orleans…owned by France at the time."

Loraine nodded. "Probably correct, Bone. These coins are uncirculated."

Silke looked down into the box. "How much do you think there is?"

Bone raised his eyebrows. "Well, that box is at least fifty pounds, and that's what?…"

"Eight hundred ounces," interrupted Haven.

"Sixteen thousand dollars, just on the price of gold bullion," offered Berkley.

Elizabeth looked up at Silke. "Is that a lot?"

Silke smiled. "You could say so, honey."

"As much as those pearls?"

She frowned, glanced quickly at Berkley, then back to Elizabeth. "Almost, honey…but not quite."

"What are we goin' to do with them?" Haven looked to Bone.

"Good question, Haven…Don't want to add another fifty pounds to Ted's load…not crossing the *Llano Estacado*, so I'd say we divi up with everybody gettin' equal amounts…That would be a little over eight pounds each in our saddlebags to carry…Shouldn't be a problem for our horses."

"So everyone gets around twenty-six hundred dollars?" asked Haven.

Bone nodded. "That's what it works out to. We were all here when you found the box…Everyone should share…Only fair, I guess."

Berkley glanced at Bone, then at the others. "That's just on the value of the gold. These coins are antiques and are prized by collectors…Especially in their condition…Will probably bring two or three times that through a dealer or a museum…I happen to know a dealer in Chicago. We can contact him when we get to Santa Fe."

"Works for me." Bone looked back at Berkley. "We'll split it up and Ted can carry the empty box. Some museum might want it, too."

"When do you think we can leave, Bone?" asked Silke.

He looked at the gray skies outside and the rain which had slacked to a drizzle. "The creeks and rivers in these canyons and arroyos usually go down about as fast as they go up…So, I'd look to tomorrow."

Loraine pulled at her doeskin top. "Just as well. Would like to dry out before gettin' back in the saddle…Nothing worse than a chaffed butt."

Silke nodded. "Good point there, Loraine. Wet clothes in a wet saddle will do that faster than a sneeze through a screen door."

"We would have really been wet had we not put on our slickers 'fore the rain started," added Haven.

Bone looked at Berkley and Haven. "Why don't ya'll and me go out soon as that drizzle stops and see about getting some more firewood…Cedar'll burn, wet or dry."

"We can picket the animals in just a bit so they can get some graze…Get 'em out of this cave, before they stink us out," said Silke.

Loraine had pulled the coffee pot from the panniers and was holding the open top under a stream of water running from the overhang at the opening. "Have some coffee in a bit…Lizbeth, you want to help me with breakfast?"

"Uh-huh. Be happy to, Loraine…Just tell me what you want me to do."

Thirty minutes later, Bone and Loraine had split up the gold in eight equal stacks for everyone. They all took their share and stowed it away in their respective saddlebags as Bone put the chest with the panniers to be loaded on Ted when they left.

The aroma of sizzling bacon permeated the confines of the cave. The drizzle outside had stopped and what little smoke from the fire went out through a crack in the twenty foot high ceiling.

Bone, Haven, and Berkley had hobbled the animals on some fresh green spring prairie grass outside after letting them drink their fill.

The three were spread out around the front of the cave collecting deadfall and blowdown cedar and mesquite limbs, all of which were rich in pitch and would burn well.

The river was full to its banks and still boiling with runoff—the temperature had dropped some twenty degrees with the passage of the front.

LLANO ESTACADO

Mad Jack's gang removed their slickers, shook the water from them and draped them over their horses' rumps to dry.

J.D. Burdick tightened up his chinch and turned to Kercher. "We gonna have some coffee an' breakfast 'fore we head east, Boss?"

"Naw, we'll stop 'round noontime to eat a bite an' clean our weapons. Need to make up some time…Be a tad muddy, but won't have no creeks to cross 'fore we git to the canyon…Don't give a jot or a tittle 'bout no whinin'."

"Wadn't whinin'…jest askin's all."

"Ya'll make sure yer canteens is full an' let's git gone."

§§§

CHAPTER EIGHTEEN

BAR M RANCH
NEW MEXICO

"Jake, ride into town, after breakfast, an' see as we got a answer from that telegram."

The lanky ranch foreman, Jake Tarbutton, looked up from his plate of huevos rancheros with Hatch green chile salsa over the top. "Yessum, Miz

Luz, be leavin' right after have my coffee....Needin' to git some salt blocks fer the horses, anyhoo." He looked down at the end of the long plank table at Luz McPherson. "Thinkin' Wilford's got somethin' else up his sleeve?"

She put down her heavy blue glazed ceramic mug. "What do you think?"

"I mind he's madder'n a wet hen 'bout you turnin' the tables on him with the sheriff."

"Seen any more of his men on our place?"

"Well, yessum, have. Seen some fellers up on the ridge on the far side…Run off 'fore we could git there."

"What were they doin'?"

"Couldn't tell, Ma'am. Weren't no horses up there, an' too rocky fer graze…Onliš fit fer sheep…Was a mite odd, ask me."

PALO DURO CANYON

Berkley took a sip of his after breakfast coffee as he leaned back against his saddle. "Those are interesting guns you and Bone carry, Silke…Fifty caliber, right?" He glanced over at Loraine.

"Yours, too…Don't think I've ever seen anything like them."

Silke looked at the big man. "Mine was a gift from Bone."

He nodded. "Know the manufacturer back east, Smith and Wesson. They're, uh…experimental models. Since I was in law enforcement, they thought it would be a good place to field test them…Sent two." Bone glanced back at Silke. "We were on a case together and she got the opportunity to use mine and…liked it. When you shoot someone or thing with it…they stay shot…Right, Silke?"

"Absolutely…Only takes one…an' just about anywhere you hit 'em with it…they're goin' down."

"Heard you shoot it when the renegades attacked…sounded like a cannon."

Silke grinned at Reg. "You oughta be close to it."

Loraine took hers from the holster. "Mine's called a semiautomatic…forty-five caliber. It's also an experimental. First semiautomatics were made in Germany…Holds seven rounds in the magazine…plus one in the chamber."

She hit the button on the side of the grip with her thumb to drop the magazine out and held it up for him to see. "It'll fire the eight rounds fast as I can pull the trigger…about a second and a half…maybe less. I can eject and put in a new mag in less than a second, and then fire another seven…Fifteen rounds on the target in less than three and a half seconds."

"My God in Heaven."

Loraine slammed the magazine back in, racked the slide, and safed the weapon. She pointed at it. "Got a safety here to keep it from firing accidentally if you drop it or something…I keep one in the chamber."

"It's like a small Gatling gun."

"Close." Loraine smiled showing her even white teeth. "I carry four spare magazines on my belt…When it's released, it'll go to the military and LEOs first."

"LEOs?"

"Law Enforcement Officers."

"Ah, of course."

"My sweet bride can hit what she aims at, too." Bone winked at Loraine. "And so can Silke, for that matter."

Haven got up, grabbed the coffee pot with one of her gloves and filled her cup. “Don’t suppose you can get another one of those fifty calibers, Bone?”

He shook his head and smiled at her. “Sorry, Haven…Uh, two was all they let me have.”

Elizabeth came back in the cave after being outside to check on her pony. “The river has gone down some, ya’ll…’bout a foot, I reckon.”

Bone nodded. “Thanks, Lizbeth.” He looked around at the others. “Storm came more from the north rather than the west where the headwater of the Red is. What runoff it got from the rain is it…Nothing more comin’ from the west.”

“Think we can maybe make a few miles later this afternoon, Bone?” asked Silke.

“I expect so.” He pulled out the map from his saddlebags, unfolded it and looked at it for a few seconds. “Might be a good idea to cut west toward Blue Water this side of Tule Creek, in case it’s still up too much to cross.”

Loraine glanced over at her husband. “How far to Blue Water?”

He frowned and studied the map some more. “Make it forty to fifty miles…if we cut off early.

Further without water…but think we've got enough water bags for the stock to make it that far."

Later that day, after the noon meal, Bone led the group along the river to the confluence with Tule Creek from the west.

He held his hand up, pulled rein, dismounted and checked Hildebrandt's girth. "Figured it would be still a little too high to try to cross, especially for Lizbeth and Calico…Safer to just head west along the creek for the next ten miles before we have to cross the *Llano*."

Loraine stepped down from Sweet Face. "We gonna camp where we have to leave the creek?"

"I'd say, Babe." He led Hildebrandt over to the edge of the muddy creek and let him drink his fill.

The others followed suit, they remounted and turned west.

Bear Dog moved out in front of them and disappeared in the mesquite and shinnery with his long-legged lope.

LLANO ESTACADO

Mad Jack Kercher's gang pulled up in an area known as South Tule Draw. "Let's camp in these trees…Don't want to run into 'em out in the open."

The copse of trees, a mix of pecan, hickory, sycamore, and oak up on a rise bordering the draw on the north, would provide good cover against anyone coming from the east.

"Bet we kin see their fire tonight from here." Ace dismounted and looked off to the east.

"Gate swings both ways, Ace," commented Burdick.

"Not if we bank it up good behind a big tree er blowdown…Water yer animals 'fore we picket 'em out…Ain't had none since this mornin'. Don't let 'em drink too fast…Damn shore don't need no foundered horses." Kercher started pulling his tack.

"Who gits first watch, Jack?"

"Funny you bring that up, Luke…"

"Aw, Jack…"

He looked around the area. "See that big pecan yonder close to the draw?"

Luke turned. "Yeah, what about it?"

"Sling yer rope 'round that big limb on the side an' clamber up there…Kin see further thataway an' down if they're in a coolie er somethin'."

Luke looked at the tree and the big limb, twenty feet off the ground. "What if'n I fall?"

Jack glared at him.

He ducked his head. "Right."

The big yellow orb settled toward the western horizon as Bone's group reined up where Tule Creek made a sharp loop to the north.

Bone glanced at the flat ground to their left, south and west, then at the gully cut by the creek on the right. "Good a place as any."

"Up here on top?" Haven dismounted.

"Nope, no need in advertising our presence. Think we're out of range of the renegades, but Bodie said there were some owlhoot gangs that roamed the area…We'll build our fire and camp down there." Bone pointed down in the arroyo. "Only ten feet or so deep."

"Good thought, Bone," said Berkley.

"Hobble the horses up here?" asked Silke.

Bone nodded. "After we water them and unload our truck down in the bottom…Bring them back up where there's good grass."

"You think they'll be all right up here? What if some of those Indians followed us to try to steal them?"

Bone grinned and pointed at Bear Dog as he climbed over the lip of the gully and padded over to the group where he and the mule touched noses. "He'll stick with Ted, Babe…Don't think anybody will bother them."

Loraine smiled back at Bone. "Oh, good point."

They led the horses and Ted down an old buffalo cut in the side of the draw to the bottom where they pulled their tack and unloaded the panniers.

The creek at the bottom of the one hundred foot wide ravine this far upstream was only fifteen to twenty feet across and had slowed precipitously.

"We'll gather some firewood when we bring the stock back up to hobble."

"Can I help, Bone?"

He smiled. "Yes, Lizbeth, you sure can."

Thirty minutes later in the gloaming, the camp fire was blazing down near the creek. Loraine stirred the beans in one skillet—Silke helped by turning the hot water cornbread patties in sizzling bacon grease in the other.

Bone glanced up at the stars as they twinkled into view from east to west. "No moon till later…Be a dark night early on."

Five miles further upstream, Luke Brown flipped his rope up over the thick limb and took his boots off so he wouldn't slip on the bark with the slick leather bottoms. He held on to the lariat and climbed his way up the side of the two foot diameter pecan tree.

Luke put his foot on the stub of a smaller limb that had broken off in times past, stood up and threw his other leg over the big one above it. He leaned back against the trunk as he straddled the limb his rope was looped around and blew out his breath.

The glow of the setting sun below the western horizon was almost gone as he peered off to the east in the growing Stygian darkness.

The night creatures, frogs, crickets, squirrels, and birds tuned up—then the screech of a night owl in the tree just above him startled the outlaw and he almost lost his grip on the branch.

"Dangnation." When he looked back to the blackness in the east, he muttered, "Well, I'll be dipped…that ain't a camp far…God's a possum."

§§§

CHAPTER NINETEEN

LLANO ESTACADO

Bone pitched the dregs of his coffee in the fire where it sizzled and popped on a burning piece of driftwood, sending up a cloud of steam—he looked over at Loraine. "Want to help me grain the horses and Ted, Babe?"

She got to her feet. "Sure, need to walk off some of those beans and cornbread, anyway."

Bone grabbed the canvas nosebags, handed three of the seven to Loraine, and they put a couple handfuls of oats mixed with cracked corn in each.

They made their way up the buffalo cut in the side of the draw to the top where the stock was hobbled on some spring grass.

All their heads snapped up, ears forward, and there were *huh...huh...huh* chuckles from most of the animals in anticipation of the feed.

Bear Dog smelled the hot water cornbread patties Loraine carried and padded over to her. She pitched one in the air and smiled as he jumped up to snatch it at its apex. He promptly laid down to munch on the hand-sized delicacy.

"Finish that one…got another for you."

He looked up at Loraine and gave her his grin, then went back to biting off chunks of the bacon fried cornmeal mush.

Bone slipped the first bag over Ted's ears, then Hildebrandt's, *d'Artagnan's*, and finally Berkley's blood bay gelding.

Loraine hung the remaining three on her mare, Sweet Face, Silke's *Lakná*, and Elizabeth's paint,

Calico. When she had finished, she turned to see Bear Dog standing looking at her, his head cocked, for his other patty. She pitched it up for him to repeat his previous action.

Bone stepped up beside Loraine. "Let's go for a little walk, Babe. They'll be done with the grain by the time we get back."

"Sounds good."

They held each other's hand as they strolled west along the rim of the arroyo.

"Gotta say, Babe…" He looked up at the myriad specks of light overhead.

"What's that?"

"There's one thing we have here in this time that we sure don't have back in ours." Bone slipped his arm around her shoulders as they continued to stroll.

"That would be?"

He pointed up with his other hand. "That…No way we have a view like that…"

Loraine looked up. "Oh, my, yes…It is breathtaking, isn't it?…It looks like there's twice or three times more stars than in our time."

He nodded. "That's what light pollution…not to say anything about what atmospheric pollution does…It's amazing all the nighttime lights of civilization, almost all over the globe, we could see when we were up in that *Anunnaki* fighter ship battling the Reptoids from *Alpha Draconia* with the Black Eagle Force." *

"I remember…No wonder we can't see anything." She leaned into his side. "I do like it here…so uncomplicated, even without indoor plumbing."

"It's comin' soon…Heard Fiona telling Mason she wanted a water closet in that rock house they moved into on the land they bought from Robert and Susan Manier."

"Oh, that's right, it adjoins the land you and Padrino got from Lucy in 2014."

"Told Stella and Peach to go buy it for us with some of that gold and diamonds she left, if we decide to go back…Need to check with them next time we go visit Lucy and get near the electromagnetic vortex."

"When we get back to Gainesville after delivering Elizabeth to her grandmother, you mean?"

He nodded.

Loraine looked up at him since his 6’8” in height towered over her 5'3". “I love you, Darrell Ulysses Bone.”

“I love you too, Loraine Maria Bone.”

She threw her arms about his neck as he lifted her up off the ground and kissed him passionately.

* *Black Eagle Force: Aurora Invasion* - Sept. 2014, amazon.com/dp/B00N01SVUC

Mad Jack looked up from where he was sitting having a late evening cup of coffee as Luke limped into the brigand’s camp.

“What’n hell happened to you?”

“Uh, I seen a kinda glow off to the east…an’ got excited when I wuz climbin’ down an’ fergot to hold both ends of the rope.”

J.D. and Ace both hoorawed Luke while Jack just shook his head.

“Yer ‘bout two shots short of bein’ a empty bottle, ain’tcha, Luke?”

“Well, hey, thankee, Boss, thankee kindly.”

“How far you reckon it was?”

Luke frowned. “Hard to tell…Just seen a little bitty bit of a glow, like I said…Coulda been down in the draw, my guess, an' anywhere from two to five miles…Night does funny things to lookin' at stuff."

J.D. pulled his twist of Brown's Mule from his pocket, cut a chunk and stuffed it in his jaw. "He's right 'bout that, Boss. Couldn't be nothin' else but a far that direction, though." He wallowed the chaw around in his cheek getting it loosened up.

Kercher nodded. "My thinkin'." He paused a moment, then looked at Ace and J.D. "Tell ya'll what do, boys. You two git yer horses an' we'll ride til we think we're gittin' closter, then git off an' slip up, kindly quiet like…an' see what's what."

Ace nodded. "Sounds good."

"We'll leave clumsy here to git over fallin' outta that tree."

Luke hung his head. "Didn't do it apurpose, Jack…wuz in a hurry to come tell yuh."

"I know." He picked up his saddle and gear and headed toward the horses.

Ace and Burdick got to their feet and carried their tack over to the horses with Mad Jack.

Bone and Loraine walked into camp from up topside. They brought the empty nosebags and put them back in the panniers.

"Enjoy your walk?" asked Silke.

Loraine smiled. "It was wonderful. You can see forever up there away from the fire…Quiet and peaceful…just the night critters." She glanced at Bone and smiled.

He nodded. "Ought to give it a try."

Silke got to her feet. "Believe I will. Used to do that a lot when I was workin' with Red Wolf."

Haven also stood. "Go with you."

"Can I go too?"

"Certainly, Lizbeth," replied Silke.

"You ladies be careful," said Berkley.

Silke looked around. "Where's Bear Dog? Thought he went with ya'll?"

Bone nodded. "Did. Took off back to the east while we were up there…Probably gone huntin'. Those corn dodgers didn't go far enough, I'd say."

Silke smiled. "True…Bet he comes trottin' back in with a jackrabbit in his mouth…grinnin' like he's done somethin'."

"Wouldn't be surprised." Bone picked up the coffee pot and shook it. "Ya'll could have left us some."

"Oops…My fault. I was the last to fill my cup."

Loraine took the pot from Bone. "Not to worry, Haven, I'll make a batch."

Bone grinned. "Well, thanks, Babe…didn't want to ask."

She frowned. "Of course you didn't…Yours tastes like you washed your socks and underwear in the water first anyway."

He feigned looking hurt, then winked at the girls as they turned and moved to the trail up to the top—all, including Elizabeth, grinning and shaking their heads.

Elizabeth stepped over to pet Calico for a moment, then ran to catch up to Silke and Haven.

The three strolled to the west along the lip of the draw, marveling at the clarity of the sky and the multitudinous stars.

"Oh, look! What are those seven real bright stars yonder called, Silke?"

She looked where the little girl was pointing. "They're called the *Pleiades* or Seven Sisters, Lizbeth. The ancient Greeks named it that...Means to sail...'cause they used them to help navigate the Mediterranean Sea."

"How do you know all that stuff, Silke?"

"My mother was a school teacher. Taught Latin and world history." She smiled. "Made sure I studied it...My name is derived from the Latin name of Cecilia...meaning Heavenly."

"And my parents...My daddy an' Silke's daddy were brothers...Named me after Silke, but used the name *Haven*, which also means, Heavenly."

"What does my name mean?"

Silke smiled. "Elizabeth is from the Hebrew name *Elisheva* in the Bible, meaning 'My God is bountiful'...and that certainly seems to be the case as far as you're concerned...I mean with all those pearls an' now the gold."

"That's just what we want to know about, girls."

Mad Jack stepped out from behind a juniper at the side of the trail in front of the three in the pale starlight—his .45 leveled at them. Ace and J.D. followed behind him and separated—guns also drawn. Ace moved to the rear.

Silke and Haven glanced behind them at the sound of Ace Cole cocking his Colt.

"You're makin' a big mistake," said Silke.

Jack chuckled. "No, missy, it's you that'll be makin' the mistake you don't take us down to your camp an' give us those pearls an' that gold you just mentioned…Didn't know 'bout that." He pointed his gun at Elizabeth. "Now, you don't want this little girl gittin' hurt…do yuh?"

Silke pulled Elizabeth close to her. "Leave her alone…You can have it all."

"Now, yer bein' sensible."

The silence was broken by the sound of two heavy bodies colliding followed immediately by a scream from Ace as he was driven forward into Silke's back along with snarls from Bear Dog.

Ace's gun discharged into the ground as Bear Dog latched on to the back of his neck, taking him on to the ground.

Silke stumbled into Mad Jack and fell to her knees.

He staggered back, but reached forward, grabbed a stunned Elizabeth, turned and disappeared into the darkness as Haven drew her

.38-40 and fired into the middle of Burdick's stomach.

J.D. cried out in pain as he collapsed to the dirt in a fetal position.

Bone, Loraine, and Berkley shot to their feet down at the camp at the cacophony of sounds from the conflict above and scrambled up the embankment.

At the top, they sprinted toward the noise of Bear Dog mauling Ace and the man's screams—they abruptly stopped with the audible sounds of bones crunching.

They could hear a horse galloping off in the distance.

The trio ran up to the scene to see dim images, in the starlit darkness, of Silke getting to her feet and Haven standing over a man moaning and writhing on the ground in front of her.

Bear Dog growled low in his throat as he straddled a very still body, which lay face down in the trail in a puddle of blood—the back of the robber's neck torn out.

Bone quickly took the event in. "Where's Lizbeth?"

Silke shook her head, pursed her lips, and pointed to the west. “One of them took her.”

§§§

CHAPTER TWENTY

LLANO ESTACADO

Bone carried a groaning Burdick down to the camp. He laid him next to the fire, looked at the others, shook his head, and mouthed, “Ain’t gonna make it…Liver shot.” He pointed at the dark, almost black, blood that soaked the front of the outlaws’ shirt on his right side.

Silke knelt down beside the mortally wounded man and leaned forward. "Where's your camp?"

J.D. gritted his teeth against the pain and looked up at her. "Up…up the…the draw…'bout five…five miles."

Bone bent over as Silke got back to her feet. "Who put ya'll up to this?…Just as well tell us, pard…Might help with your maker some."

"They knew about the pearls, Bone, an' where we'd be…But didn't know about the gold till the leader heard me mention it 'fore they stepped out from behind a cedar tree."

Bone nodded at Silke.

Burdick glanced, reached one hand up and grabbed the front of Bone's shirt. "Dyin'…ain't I?"

"Sure's you're born, slick…Don't have long. Best make your peace."

Burdick moaned louder with a stab of pain, released Bone's shirt and arched his back.

"Who sent you?"

His wild agony filled eyes looked around at the others, rested on Berkley a moment, then back to Bone. "It was…it was…ahhh."

Burdick sighed out his death rattle as his entire body relaxed—his eyes dilated and fixed in a sightless stare at Bone—left heel briefly hammering a staccato on the ground.

Bone looked up at Loraine and pursed his lips. "Close, but no cigar."

He got to his feet as they heard the sound of a horse galloping away. "Oh, damn, Silke's going after Elizabeth."

Bone strode over to his gear, picked up his saddle and pad and clambered up the cut in the side of the arroyo.

"You'll never catch her on Hildebrandt," said Loraine.

"I know."

"I'll go, too." Berkley walked over to his tack.

Bone stopped halfway up the embankment and turned. "No…Got a better chance by myself…it's what I do." He turned back and disappeared over the top of the draw.

Silke and her sure-footed Indian pony, *Issoba Lakná*, galloped across the flat plain of the *Llano* in the starlit darkness with Bear Dog running tirelessly alongside. Her long, thick strawberry blonde hair flowed in the wind behind her like diaphanous silk. They maintained the pace for a little over a mile before she bumped the gelding back to a lope, then a trot.

Silke kept the shadowy image of the gully on her right, knowing the outlaws' camp was also in it, but according to Burdick, around five miles upstream.

When she reached what felt like four miles, Silke pulled her horse to a stop next to a copse of cedar, dismounted, and ground tied the lathered mount.

"Stay here, boy, goin' on foot."

The wolf-dog looked up at her as she loosened *Lakná's* girth so he could catch his breath while he grazed. She pulled her Winchester from the boot.

Silke walked over to South Tule Draw and found a place to clamber down the eight foot embankment to the bottom, followed by Bear Dog.

Tule Creek was only ten feet wide at this point. She turned and headed west upstream slowly in the darkness, keeping her eyes peeled for the glow of a campfire ahead.

The first bend in the draw rewarded her with what she sought. Her Apache style knee-high moccasins made little to no sound as she toe-heeled toward the light.

Silke eased up behind some shinnery that grew along the stream and squatted down. A low rumble came from Bear Dog's throat as he flattened himself lower to the sandy floor of the draw. She could see Elizabeth sitting between two men on the far side of the fire—a blanket draped around her shoulders.

"So where's the stuff?" Mad Jack leaned over her, his hands on his thighs.

Bone trotted the massive Hildebrandt along the same direction as Silke. He saw the black half-Friesian's ears flick to their right and reined up—the gelding nickered.

An answering whinny came from the darkness near the draw. He reined over in that direction and they walked up to *Lakná* munching on some of the short, curly, spring buffalo grass. The two horses touched noses and chuckled down in their throats at each other's familiarity.

Bone dismounted, dropping his reins to the ground, and also loosened the big horse's cinch before turning and heading to the arroyo.

He partially slid down the embankment to the floor of the draw, crouched and headed west almost at a jog, thankful he had not looked at the fire back at camp. His night vision was at an optimum.

Silke leaned her rifle against a juniper, removed the hammer thong from her 500 and drew the big gun with her right hand. She pulled the tomahawk from her belt with her left, held it down alongside her leg, and stepped out into the edge of the campfire light.

Bear Dog crouched at her side, his blue eyes glinted red from the reflection of the fire—ready to charge the two men, his lips pulled back in a snarl.

"Don't move, don't even twitch or you'll die where you stand." She pointed the hand cannon at Mad Jack.

His gaze jerked from Elizabeth to the figure at the edge of the campfire light as she stepped out from behind the brush. "What the…"

Luke also turned to look at the Pinkerton—he glanced at Kercher. "Boss?"

"Shut up." His lips curled up in a sneer as he looked at Silke. "You think you can take us both?"

She smiled. "Nope…Know I can. You might get one in me, but you'll both be dead."

"Bold talk…for a woman." He surreptitiously rotated his body in the flickering firelight to hide the Colt on his hip and his right hand from her vision.

"A woman who's goin' to blow you in two first…you don't be still." Her lips barely moved. "Just as soon kill you as not…Save havin' to take you in…Lizbeth, move over there." She motioned with her head to her right. "Bear Dog, go to her."

The big black half-wolf slunk over to stand between the little girl and the men as she eased to the right.

"Now, drop 'em," ordered Silke.

Jack shook his head. "Don't think so."

He and Luke reached for their guns at the same time.

The stillness of the night was shattered by three almost simultaneous explosions and blinding flashes of light that lit up the area like day for a brief second—one much bigger than the other two. Elizabeth screamed.

A big cloud of gunsmoke boiled up between Mad Jack and Luke as Bone rushed into the firelight with his .50 caliber Smith & Wesson in his hand.

The big man stopped when he saw the two outlaws on their backs. A massive blood stain in the middle of Mad Jack's chest continued to spread as his life's fluid leaked out. Luke Brown's head was split open with the entire blade of Silke's tomahawk buried up to the shaft between his eyes.

Elizabeth had both hands over her ears and was squatted down. Bear Dog stood front of her, facing the two bodies, his legs spread wide.

Bone rushed up to Silke. "You hit?"

She shook her head. "The ugly one fired over my head an' the other shot into the dirt at his own feet."

Bone looked at her, at the two men, and back at her. "You shot that one dead center with your 500 and simultaneously threw your tomahawk at the other, hitting him in the center of his forehead?" He shook his head. "Nobody's going to believe this."

Silke smiled. "Kinda don't believe it myself. They didn't leave me no choice…Good thing the skinny one was a bit slow pullin' his iron."

Bear Dog trotted over and smelled of each body, then went back to Elizabeth and sat down beside her.

"You awright, Lizbeth?" asked Silke.

She looked at the bodies, then to her. "Uh-huh."

Bone holstered his gun, stepped over and picked her up. Elizabeth wrapped her arm around his neck as she stared at the two dead men.

"Let's go back to camp."

She just nodded.

Silke went through the men's pockets and pulled out a folded yellow telegram from Jack's vest. She opened the flimsy and held it close to the fire.

"What's it say?" asked Bone. "Can you tell who it's from?"

Silke shook her head. "*Party headed to Santa Fe - stop - Have pearls - stop - Know what to do - stop*." She looked up at Bone. "It's unsigned."

"Still don't know who sent them, then…The guy at the camp died before he could tell us."

She nodded. "Figured."

Two hours later, after turning the outlaw's horses loose and caving the bank of the draw down over the bodies, Silke, Elizabeth, and Bone were back at their camp.

They worked their way down the embankment after hobbling the horses with the others again, and pulling the tack. They had watered them before leaving the outlaw camp and trotted the animals back the five miles.

Bear Dog scrambled down after them.

Loraine got to her feet. "No prisoners?"

Bone shook his head as he set Elizabeth on the ground. "Not likely. Decided they didn't want to come along…Silke took both of them out before I got there."

Loraine frowned. "Both?"

"Yeah." He grinned. "You won't believe."

"They say anything?" asked Berkley.

Silke shook her head and held up the telegram. "One of 'em had this…Doesn't say who it's from. Has the telegraph sender operator's initials, but that's it."

SILKE'S RIDE

§§§

CHAPTER TWENTY-ONE

BLUE WATER, TEXAS

Silke, Haven, Bone, Loraine, Elizabeth, and Berkley dismounted in front of Murphy's Livery on Main Street.

Bear Dog who had been riding on top of Ted's panniers, jumped down when they stopped, trotted over to the water trough, stood on his back legs, leaned over and lapped his fill.

Haven glanced next door at another sign above the awning - Murphy's Wet Goods and across the street at Murphy's Hotel. "Wonder the town's not named Murphy." She turned to Silke who was letting her horse drink at the wooden water trough. "Think it's the same guy, cuz?"

She grinned. "Would bet."

A tall, stick thin, towheaded teen in blue bib overalls and a wide-brimmed straw hat stepped out of the double-wide doors of the red livery barn. "Hep ya'll?"

Bone turned from leading Hildebrandt to the trough next to Silke and Haven's mounts. "Need to stable the animals for the night, feed and groom 'em."

The boy nodded. "Seventy-five cents each with the grain…check their feet fer yuh, too…I'm Fats Murphy." He shrugged and grinned.

Bone looked the skinny boy up and down. "Can see that."

"Started callin' me that at school when I was a kid…Stuck."

Silke grinned again. "Who'd a guessed?"

"Your pa serve meals at his saloon next door?" asked Bone.

Fats shook his head. "Nope…Ma does though. She lets Pa sell the spirits."

Loraine turned from watering Sweet Face. "You need to be on the stage."

Fats had a deadpan look on his freckled face. "Ain't one till tomorra."

Haven tried to hide her giggle as she turned away.

"Store yer truck in the office, no charge, neither," he added.

"We'll keep our saddlebags." Bone pulled his from behind his cantle and stepped over to get Elizabeth's.

Fats nodded. "Most folks usually do."

The big man smiled. "Figured."

The boy looked at Bear Dog. "That a wolf?"

"Half," replied Silke.

"Ain't never seen a blue-eyed wolf dog afore."

"Most haven't…He'll stay with the mule. They're buddies."

"Huh…Who knew?"

"Got rooms at your ma's hotel?" asked Berkley.

He cocked his head. “Uh-huh…How’d you know it was ma’s?”

“Just a wild guess.”

Bone slung his and Elizabeth’s heavy saddlebags over his broad shoulder. “Shall we go see what Miz Murphy has to eat?”

Silke got her bags. “Thought you’d never bring it up. Figured ya’ll were gonna palaver the rest of the day.”

Bone shook his head and mumbled as he led off toward Murphy’s Wet Goods, “Ten thousand comedians looking for a job of work and everybody’s trying to be one.”

They pushed through the batwing doors and waited a few moments for their eyes to adjust to the dim light. It wasn’t bad this late in the afternoon with the sunlight coming in the two large multi-paned glass windows in the front.

Bone pointed at a large round table near the back wall, far enough from the rinky-tink piano so they could converse.

The derby-decked piano player was banging out a lively rendition of Scott Joplin’s, *Maple Leaf Rag*.

Loraine glanced over at the Hoagy Carmichael look alike playing. “Wow, he’s good.”

Bone nodded. “Makes you want to dance.”

His wife grinned and punched his arm. “Try to get over it, Bone…Please.”

“You kiddin’ me, Babe?…I’m twinkle toes.”

“Yeah, like a wounded buffalo.”

Bone grimaced. “Ouch.”

The potbellied bartender walked up to their table. “What’ll it be, folks?…I’m Murphy.”

Haven shook her head. “Would’ve never guessed.”

He glanced over at her. “How’s that?”

“Nothin’…What’s on the menu?”

“Let me get Ma.” He walked to the door next to the bar and stuck his head in. “Got some folks out here want to eat, dear.”

A Ma Kettle type of woman came out of the kitchen, wiping her hands on a dish towel. “Evenin’ folks. Pa tells me you’re hungry?”

Bone nodded. “My stomach thinks my throat’s been cut.”

She looked over at him. “At your size, how would it know?”

He laughed. "What is it with this town? Everybody cracks jokes."

She looked at Bone. "Who's jokin'?"

Bone wisely held back a comment. "We'd like to order."

"I'm Phoebe, most call me Ma, you'll eat what I got an' like it."

"And that is?" asked Silke.

"Chicken'n dumplin's or steak an' taters, yer choice…Apple cobbler for desert."

Bone went first, "Smelled the cobbler when we walked in…Steak for me…what kind of potatoes?"

She frowned at him and slapped an ample thigh with her towel.

He nodded. "Yeah…What you got."

Silke looked at Elizabeth next to her. "Honey?"

"I'd like the chicken'n dumplin's, please an' thank you."

"My, aren't you polite?…Would you like a glass of fresh milk with that?"

"Yes, Ma'am." A big grin spread across her face.

"Love a polite child." She looked at Silke.

"Steak for me, too."

"Two steaks." Her gaze went to Loraine.

"Steak."

"That's three."

"I'll have the chicken'n dumplin's, please Ma'am," said Haven.

Phoebe looked at Silke and back to Haven. "Ya'll sisters?"

"Cousins."

"Look enough alike to be twins, 'cept fer the hair." Her gaze moved to Berkley. "Let me guess…Steak?"

He nodded. "Very good, Madam."

"You had that look. "Four steaks an' two chickens…Be back in a bit."

Bone held up his hand. "Could we have some coffee now while we wait?"

She sighed. "Ask Franklin. He handles the drinks." Phobe turned on her heel and strode back to her kitchen.

Bone shook his head. "Don't believe it."

Loraine frowned and looked at him. "Believe what?"

"Her name is Phobe and her husband is Franklin…The same as Ma and Pa Kettle."

"Who's Ma and Pa Kettle?" asked Silke.

Loraine kicked Bone's shin.

He grimaced, looked at Berkley, and turned to Silke. "Uh…they're play actors back home, Marjorie Main and Percy Kilbride, that play comedy characters, Ma and Pa Kettle, in, uh…vaudville and that new thing called moving pictures."

"Oh, that Kinetoscope thing of Edison's."

Bone nodded. "Yeah, that's it…It would make a good investment."

"Gave it some thought…Think it's a fad. Just don't believe it's going to last."

"You might be surprised," muttered Bone.

"How's that?" Berkley cupped his hand behind his ear because of the piano.

Bone held up his hand and signaled to Murphy. "Nothing…Anybody want coffee?"

Everyone at the table, but Elizabeth, nodded.

A wry grin spread across Berkley's face. "Glad I didn't say medium rare on my steak."

Loraine's eyebrows arched. "You might have left wearing it instead of eating it."

He nodded. "Exactly."

Murphy strolled over.

Bone held up five fingers. "Five coffees please…you don't mind."

"Be right back."

Berkley turned to Silke. "You mind if I ask you a question?"

She nodded. "Answer if I can."

"Back in camp, when that robber died, you mentioned something about him knowing about the pearls?"

She glanced at Haven. "Elizabeth inherited around two pounds of fresh water pearls, white, tan, blue, and wine colored from her uncle. She's taking one of the wine ones we had mounted for her grandmother in Santa Fe."

"Oh, how nice…So you're carrying all those pearls around with you? They must be worth a fortune."

Silke shook her head. "Oh, goodness me, no…We left them with Bone's godfather back in Gainesville. Would have never tried to carry them with us."

He nodded. "Ah, that's good thinking…Wonder how the outlaws knew about them?"

Silke and Haven exchanged glances again. "That's what we were wondering."

Berkley cocked his head. "Who all knew?"

She pursed her full lips. "Actually, quite a few people back in Gainesville…The town marshal and a group of teenagers, the banker, our landlady at the boarding house where we live…along with the other guests, and a local jeweler." Silke frowned and studied Berkley briefly. "And a man who was in the jewelry shop when we were having the one mounted for Lizbeth's grandmother an' seein' if we could get rest of them appraised…Just didn't pay much attention to him."

Berkley's skin flushed briefly.

Murphy came back with a tray of five coffees and one milk. He set it on the table. "There you be, folks, five coffees with cream an' sugar…Ma sent out the milk for the little lady."

§§§

CHAPTER TWENTY-TWO

BAR M RANCH
NEW MEXICO

The plump Mexican ranch cook filled Jake's coffee cup and took his empty breakfast plate away.

"*Gracias*, Martina."

"*No hay nada que agradecer*, *S*eñor Jake." She then disappeared into the kitchen.

"Don't know why there wadn't no answer from my boys at the Western Union and Cable office?" Luz McPherson, at the end of the big plank table took a sip from her heavy blue stoneware mug and set it back on the table.

"Mebe they jest hit the trail, not thinkin' 'bout sendin' a reply…be halfway here by now, reckon."

Luz nodded. "Could be right…Know in 'bout a week, then." She held her napkin to her mouth and coughed several times.

"Gittin' worse, Miz Luz?"

She nodded. "Comes an' goes…Rain shower we had yesterd'y didn't help none."

"Yessum."

"Take a couple of the boys out an' go check that ridge again today, Jake. Wanta know what the hell it is they're interested in out there…Completely 'cross my place from their line."

"Yessum, makes three times we've seen 'em there."

"What I mean."

"Ben Wilford's slicker'n a boiled onion…wouldn't trust him any further than I can chunk 'im."

"Well, we're fixin' to start raisin' hell an' stick a chunk under it when my boys git here."

BLUE WATER, TEXAS

Bone lifted a bubble in his saddle blanket under the gullet of his saddle, pulled the slack from his latigo and threaded it back through the loop. He snapped it down, lifted the two inch leather-wrapped stirrup from the saddlehorn and let it fall to Hildebrandt's side.

"Water bags full, Fats?" Bone glanced over at the young hostler as he was saddling Calico for Elizabeth.

"Yessir, put fresh water in all of 'em an' filled yer canteens, too…Purty good stretch cross the *Llano* 'fore you git to Ragtown in New Mexico…Most of a hunderd mile, reckon."

"You're a good man, Fats." He pitched him a ten dollar gold piece. "Something extra for your work…Ragtown's this side of Tucumcari Mountain, right?"

Fats snatched the coin from the air, looked at it, put a small dent in both sides when he bit down on it and grinned. "Wow, thank you Mister Bone...Yessir, sure is."

"And it's just Bone, son. Mister Bone was my daddy."

"Yessir."

"Tell your ma she makes just about the best buttermilk pancakes I ever had."

Silke stabbed a toe into her stirrup and swung easily up in her saddle. "I'll go double on that." She shifted her weight to the right to re-center her saddle.

Fats lifted Elizabeth up, set her in Calico's saddle and handed her the reins.

"Yessir, tell her that, but 'magine she already knows."

Loraine laughed as she also set her saddle straight. "Bet she does."

Haven and Berkley mounted up and followed Bone, leading Ted down the street to the west and out on the Staked Plains. Bear Dog padded alongside the mule.

Loraine trotted up next to Bone. "Never heard of Ragtown, New Mexico."

He grinned and glanced at her. "They change the name to Tucumcari, in 1908..."

Silke trotted up on the other side of Bone. “What’s this about Ragtown?”

Bone glanced back over his shoulder at Berkley riding beside Elizabeth and Haven about ten yards back. He turned to Silke.

“In our time, Ragtown is known as Tucumcari…but between now and 1908, it’s known as Six Shooter Station because of all the gunfights there as virtue of the Chicago, Rock Island and Pacific Railroad finishing the line into that part of New Mexico next year.”

Silke raised her well-shaped eyebrows. “Oh, joy.”

Bone grinned. “That bother you?”

She shook her head. “Not my first rodeo, Bone.”

RAGTOWN, NEW MEXICO

Three days later at sundown, the dusty and tired group walked their jaded mounts into the village and trading post of Ragtown after an uneventful passage across the *Llano Estacado*.

They reined up and dismounted at the full water tank below the windmill next to the combination trading post and saloon—loosened their girths and let the animals drink their fill of the cool, clear water. There was no danger of foundering as they had walked the tired horses and Ted the last five miles and they weren't hot.

Bone removed his Jack Bull hat and stuck his head under the water. He raised up after ten seconds or so and shook the excess water from his short cropped hair.

"Ooo, that felt good." He looked on the other side of the trading post. "Got a Chinese laundry…bet a dollar they got baths in the back."

Loraine splashed some water in her face. "Would love a hot bath to scrape this trail dust off and get my under things washed."

"Oh, me too," joined in Silke and Haven almost at the same time.

Silke looked down at Elizabeth. "Would you like a hot bath, Honey?"

"Oh, yes, please."

Berkley tried to brush some of the dust from his coat. "I do hope they can get these trail clothes clean."

Loraine grinned. "Seen them work wonders cleaning as well as mending…The Chinese laundry in Jacksboro, mended up some gunshot holes and you couldn't even tell where they had been."

They let the animals finish and led them down to Dooley's Livery and Feed on the other side of the laundry.

A seedy fifty year old man in dirty canvas pants, suspenders, red longjohn top, and a misshapen brown fedora, with pale red hair sticking out from under it, stepped out from the front of the dark green board and batt barn.

He pulled a well-used corncob pipe from his mouth. "How do?...Fergus Dooley's the moniker. Is it stallin' an' feed fer ye tired and woebegone stock ye be seekin', then ye've come to the right place..." He chuckled. "The *only* place till ye be gettin' to Las Vegas...fer as that goes."

Bone stepped down from his saddle and stretched his back. "Well, Mister Dooley, that we do, that we do. Stall, feed and a good rub down."

"Seventy-five cents each. I'll be givin' ye a two-bit discount fer the seven animals...be an even five dollars. Throw in any shoein', if needed."

"Sounds like a deal." Bone pointed at Bear Dog. "He'll stay with the mule."

"Figured...Could tell they was 'tached. He'll be watchin' yer gear, I'm takin' it?"

"You take right," said Silke. "Don't think you'll have to worry about anybody botherin' it."

"It's good to know, that is...It's some real ne'er-do-wells we got round here."

Loraine pulled her saddlebags from Sweet Face. "Got baths at the Chinese place?"

He nodded. "Do...Change the water at sundown, so it's fresh water ye'll be gettin'."

She grinned. "Thank the Lord for small favors."

Bone touched the brim of his hat. "Be leavin' about daylight, Shamus."

"It's Fergus, an' it's fed and ready they'll be."

They turned and headed to the laundry next door. A hand-painted sign over the half glass door read: ZHANG WEI'S LAUNDRY EMPORIUM.

Bone held the door open for the others. A two inch brass bell attached to the header tinkled when he opened it.

A small Chinese man wearing a traditional red silk cheongsam and matching Chinese cap with a long black pig tail hanging out the back walked up. "Come in to *Zhang Wei's*...you velly velcome. Ve Vash clothes, you vash bodies...Velly good."

Bone grinned. "We'll take both, pard. You can get our clothes when we shuck 'em back at the baths."

"Velly good. *Zhang Wei* clean. Make like new. You see. Need *Zhang Wei's* ladies vash backs? Do velly good."

"We can handle that part, pard." Bone moved toward the door to the back.

Loraine smiled at *Zhang Wei* and bowed slightly with her palms together. "*Xièxiè ni, gudài.*"

"Oh! You know Chinese customs?" asked *Zhang Wei.*

She nodded. "This unworthy one has earned a seventh level black belt in *Kung Fu* and *Wushu.*"

Zhang Wei returned her bow in the same manner. "For you, *Zhang Wei* take extra care." He nodded to his wife, also wearing a Chinese gown, to lead them to the back.

"*Xièxie,*" Loraine replied and followed the others after his wife.

Berkley turned to her as they walked through the steaming wash area that smelled strongly of lye soap to the curtained off bath area. "You speak Chinese?"

She grinned and nodded. "Only a little…Just said, 'thank you, ancient one', in Mandarin."

The diminutive Chinese woman pointed to three steaming wooden tubs on each side of the room separated by a Chinese curtain.

"You find water is hot. Soap and towels on stool next to tubs. You need help you call *Chao-xing*, I come help, velly quick…I come back and get clothes when you get in tubs."

She touched the hole in Loraine's doeskin top. "*Chao-Xing*, fix velly good. You see." She went back through the curtain to the laundry area.

"Wonder what her name means?" asked Haven. "It's pretty."

Loraine smiled. "It means, morning star…And I'll bet our clothes will be spotless and smell good, too."

Haven frowned and looked at Loraine. "How will they get them dry?"

"Did you see those three glowing potbellied stoves at the side of the room back there?"

Haven nodded.

"Not only do they heat the water on them, but they also hang the clothes around them after they get 'em washed…They'll iron 'em too."

Silke nodded, too. "Don't see how those women in there work. It was hot as blazes."

"Used to it." Loraine started pulling off her doeskins after she hung her gunbelt on a peg.

On the other side of the curtain, Bone and Berkley had removed their clothes, hung up their gunbelts and were each settling into the bathwater.

The front curtain parted as *Chao-Xing* stepped in, picked up their clothes, went through to the other side and got the girls. "They be leady soon. You bathe velly good."

"Ahhh." Bone sighed as he sunk down to his chin. "This feels so good."

Berkley glanced over at the big man's tub and the stool next to it. "See you kept that hand cannon out." He indicated the Smith & Wesson 500 on the top next to the bar of lavender scented lye soap.

"Habit."

"Think you might need it?"

"What I heard about this town, figured it's best to err on the cautious side…Folks have been known to be robbed while in the bath…Intend to see that's not a possibility. If you get my drift."

Berkley arched his eyebrows and nodded. He leaned back against the side of the tub and glanced one more time at the gun under Bone's towel.

§§§

CHAPTER TWENTY-THREE

ZHANG WEI'S LAUNDRY EMPORIUM

Bone slid further down in the steaming hot water as he felt a draft of air across his back. "Woo, that's chilly."

"It is," Berkley concurred as he did the same.

Bone turned to see why the rear door of the laundry was open. Two rough-looking men stepped in from outside, guns drawn.

"Cold air is the least of your worries, man-mountain."

The lead ruffian wearing a dark green bowler, stepped forward along the curtain dividing the men's bath from the women's.

Bone reached his hand out to lay over his towel covering his .50 cal.

"You don't need no towel, big man." He waved his Remington at Bone. "Jest stay put. "We ain't gonna be long. Seen yer little group come in from cross the street…Ya'll didn't come right out so we figured you wuz takin' baths…Them saddlebags looked a mite heavy…Be thinkin' we'll be a takin' 'em with us."

Bone grinned. "Not likely."

The bandit sneered. "Oh? Don't look to me like yer in much of a position to do much about it. The only guns ya'll got won't reach this far…Haw."

The other man also guffawed. "'Sides they're all wet." He laughed again.

"Now ya'll jest sit real still whilst we…Ahhh!"

The would-be robber arched his back as his eyes rolled up in his head and his mouth opened to take a breath—but to no avail. His knees buckled as he dropped to the damp floor like so much wet laundry, jerking the divider curtain with him.

A Chickasaw war tomahawk was buried between his shoulder blades, pinning the silken material to his back.

The roar of three loud, almost simultaneous, explosions followed as Loraine triple-tapped her .45 semiautomatic in the middle of the second man's chest less than an inch apart as he turned when the curtain dropped, sending him to the floor to join his compadre.

Bone and Berkley looked up to see Silke, Loraine, and Haven holding their towels against their wet chests.

Loraine and Haven swept the room and the back door with their pistols for any other threats while Silke had an impish grin across her face. Elizabeth looked at the two men on the floor—her wide eyes just above the lip of her tub.

Silke shrugged her shapely shoulders. "Heard 'em come in an' what they were sayin'...Didn't figure they'd expect anything from this side."

The front curtain swept aside as *Chao-Xing* and *Zhang Wei* rushed inside. He was holding a long double-barreled shotgun and his wife had a thick three foot wooden stick, used to stir clothes in the boiling wash pots, raised over her head.

"Iiieee!...*Whè shì shénme*?...*Whè shì shénme*?"

"We had a couple of men wanting our bags...We didn't think they should have them," answered Loraine.

Chao-Xing motioned to several of the wash ladies to drag the bodies outside.

Silke held up one hand. "Uh...could I have my tomahawk back before they drag them outside?"

Zhang Wei nodded and repeatedly bowed offering his profuse apologies. "So solly, so solly. *Zhang Wei* offer you baths an' laundry no charge...We so solly."

Zhang Wei leaned his shotgun against Bone's tub, stepped over to the first man's body and grabbed hold of the tomahawk handle to pull it free. It wouldn't budge. He put a sandaled foot just below the blade on the man's back and pulled on the war hatchet with both hands. At first it didn't move, then with a cracking sound, it jerked free from the split vertebra. He handed it to *Chao-Xing*.

"We clean velly good, you see…no blood." *Zhang Wei* looked down at the bloody green silk curtain wadded on the floor with the bodies. "We fix, chop-chop, velly quick." He nodded at the extra washer women who had come in through the curtain.

In a couple of short minutes, they brought in a clean replacement curtain, threaded it through the hangers and hooked it back onto the wall supports.

"Bling fresh hot water…baths get cold, chop-chop." *Zhang Wei* waved his hands, directing his employees.

An hour later, the group had dressed in fresh clothing from their saddlebags and headed out the front door.

Zhang Wei bowed several more times. "Clothes be cleaned and ironed, velly quick. We bring after you eat supper at Horse Head saloon across street.

Loraine, dressed in her camo BDUs, like Bone, pulled her dark hair back into a pony tail and slipped a scrunchie she had with her from 2018 over it. "Don't know when I've felt so clean."

Haven nodded. “Especially after scraping three inches of accumulated dirt off…had to be a major improvement…Love havin’ clean hair.” She shook her still slightly damp long raven tresses from side to side.

Silke checked her tomahawk and arched her brows. “Clean as a whistle, too.”

“Hope we don’t run into any more miscreants in the saloon,” said Berkley.

Bone frowned as they stepped up on the boardwalk in front of the saloon. “Wouldn’t count on it.”

He went through the batwing doors first, let his eyes adjust to the light, and then held them open for the others.

They made their way to a large round table that would seat all six of them as the normal saloon odors assailed their nostrils.

“The peach cobbler is almost overcoming the stink of smoke and vomit…I said almost.” Loraine grinned.

Several of the cowboys at the plank bar turned and crudely appraised the ladies.

“Well, looks like the clientele of the Horse Head is pickin’ up some.” The cowboy nudged the man next to him.

“Wonder if’n them two fellers be needin’ some help?” asked the other.

The first man spat a long stream of tobacco juice at the spittoon near his foot, missing most of it. “Curt an’ Gomer’ll be upset they missed out.

Bone, overhearing their lightly veiled comments, got back to his feet. “Be right back, ya’ll…Need to nip something in the bud.”

He stepped up to the two loudmouths. “Boys, did one of your runnin’ buddies you just mentioned have a dark green bowler and the other wearing a pair of chaps that had seen better days?”

The first man nodded. “Why, shore, ya’ll met ‘em, did yuh?” He looked at his friend and grinned. “They’re a couple of real curly wolves, them two.”

Bone grinned. “You could say so. Seems they tried to rob us while we were indisposed in the bath across the street.” He turned and pointed at Silke and Loraine. “Now two of those sweet looking ladies…and one of them is my wife…you fellows were ogling over there, killed the both of them before they could bat their eyes…The one with the light colored hair took good ol' Curt out with her tomahawk and my wife put three rounds in the center of Gomer's chest you could cover with one hand."

"Huh?" said the first man.

"Yer funnin' us," added the other.

Bone shook his head and grinned. "Not tonight." He slipped his massive arms around the shoulders of the two and pulled them close with a little more force than was needed.

The two men groaned as Bone squeezed them hard enough to make their bones pop.

He lowered his voice, "Now, I'm going to suggest ya'll mind your Ps and Qs while we're eating and I'll do my dead level best to keep them from adding you two to their tally, oh, and that younger one with the long raven hair got left out of the activities and she's real upset about it…Now I wouldn't say she was on the prod, but then again, I wouldn't say she wasn't…Ya'll follow what I'm saying?"

The first man swallowed his chaw and coughed. "Why, shore, we wuz jest goin' on, didn't mean no harm…Ain't that right, Slim?"

"Uh-huh." He nodded as he tried to get his breath.

Bone released his vise-like grip, patted the men on their shoulders, and looked up at the wide-eyed bartender. "Give these boys a couple of beers…on me." He glanced back at the cowboys. "You boys have a nice evenin'…hear?"

Bone turned and walked back to the table and sat back down.

Loraine leaned over. "What did you say to them?"

He shrugged his shoulders. "Oh, not much, babe, just that they'd have a much more pleasant evening if they minded their own business."

The bartender sauntered over to their table. "Nice work over there, big man. Them two were needin' a little straightenin' up…So, what'll it be, folks?…Got some fresh elk stew with Hatch chilies an' hot flour tortillas."

Bone nodded. "Sounds good to me." He glanced at everyone and got nodded agreements. "All the way around…Bring the little girl some milk, you got it."

"Comin' right up."

NEW MEXICO TERRITORY

Two days later after spending the night in Ragtown above the Horse Head, and giving the stock a much needed rest, they trotted up to the springs at Twelve Mile Creek known as Apache Springs.

Bone dismounted from Hildebrandt. "Be our last camp before Santa Fe."

Silke followed suit. "How much further, Bone?"

"I make it forty miles or so and another two thousand feet in altitude…give or take."

"Know what we are here?" asked Haven.

Berkley pulled the tack from his gelding. "I can answer that…kind of my bailiwick. We're right at five thousand feet here and Santa Fe is a little over seven thousand feet. We've been going uphill since we left Ragtown."

Loraine grinned and rubbed her bottom. "I can tell."

They looked off to the northwest at the peaks of the mountains.

Elizabeth pointed. "What are those mountains called?"

Berkley looked at her and smiled. "The *Sangre de Cristo* Mountains…means the blood of Christ…They were named by the Spanish explorer *Antonio Valverde y Cosio* in 1719, when he saw the morning sun on the snowy peaks. It is said, he muttered, '*Sangre de Cristo*'." He smiled. "Had to learn about the area when I was studying geology in college."

Silke set her saddle, blanket, saddlebags, and bedroll near a ring of rocks established by some previous travelers. "When will you be leavin' us, Mister Berkley?"

"Oh, I'll cut west about five miles out of Santa Fe. I have a client that owns a horse ranch in that direction…The Circle W."

§§§

CHAPTER TWENTY-FOUR

APACHE SPRINGS

The night sounds of frogs, owls, crickets, and a distant pack of coyotes tuning up, joined with the gurgling of the spring filled the area around the camp. A new moon crested the eastern horizon.

Berkley took his plate of beans with bacon and wild onions, and cornbread—moved over to sit beside Elizabeth on a log at the edge of the campfire light.

Bone and Loraine sat on large rocks near their bedrolls while Silke and Haven ate cross-legged Indian style on their blankets.

"Be glad to get there, babe?"

Loraine looked askance at Bone. "I'll be glad to get anywhere…But it is really pretty here and beats the *Llano*."

He got to his feet, picked up another couple of pieces of deadfall and threw them on the fire, sending a shower of crackling sparks curling up into the cool night air.

"Gettin' a bit nippy, too."

"We're in the mountains, Bone."

"I knew that…Just testing you."

"Oh, look." Loraine pointed to a spot of light streaking across the sky. "Meteor."

"You sure? Tell me, is there a fire tail and is it headed toward the ground?"

She looked again. "No."

"Then I'll bet you it's one of Lucy's friends."

"You think?"

"We're not too far north of that Ley line that runs through Roswell and Aurora, Texas."

She stared as the speck made an impossible ninety degree right turn to the north and disappeared in the blink of an eye.

"Wow, could be." She looked over as Bear Dog trotted into camp with a large jack rabbit in his jaws. "Looks like he's got his supper, too."

Berkley held a rock up to Elizabeth. "This is what's known as an igneous rock. There are basically three kinds of rock...sedimentary...it's laid down in layers over thousands of years, mostly in water...Then metamorphic, which is sedimentary or conglomerate rock that's been under a lot of pressure under the earth over millions of years...and..." He turned the hard dark rock over in his hand. "Finally...igneous...It's formed way inside the earth where everything is hot and melted and brought to the surface by geologic upheavals and volcanos."

"Are there volcanos in New Mexico?"

"Well, honey, there used to be...Used to be a lot of them, and they poured molten rock out upon the ground known as 'lava', which can form all sorts of other rocks...It can also have a lot of things in it from silver and gold to precious stones like sapphires, emeralds, turquoise, rubies, and in some parts of the world…diamonds."

"Are there any in that rock?" She pointed to the one in his hand.

He smiled, pitched it up in his hand and caught it. "No, not in this one."

Haven glanced over at Berkley and Elizabeth. "Noticed how he seems to be spending more time with Lizbeth?"

Silke glanced at them. "She likes him and she's been askin' a lot of questions about rocks an' stuff."

Haven nodded. "The curiosity of a child."

"True."

The morning broke crisp and cold with a light coating of frost on the spring grass as Loraine stirred the coals back to life. She added a number of small dry branches, and then a couple of larger ones before she stepped over to the spring to fill the coffee pot.

Bone rolled out of his blankets, shook his tall moccasins and pulled them on before he got to his feet. "I'll water the guys and your mare so they'll be ready to go after we finish breakfast."

Haven stepped over from her bedroll. "Give you a hand, Bone."

"Help always appreciated, missy."

"One more hand wouldn't hurt, would it?" asked Berkley. "Got seven head to water."

"Beats making two trips, Reg," said Bone. "Ya'll take two each, I'll get three."

They removed the hobbles, then led the stock over to the babbling stream flowing downhill out of the spring and let them drink their fill of the cold, clear mountain water.

An hour later after they had finished breakfast, loaded up and cleaned their campsite, Bone led the group along the narrow path that climbed up the side of the mountain.

Silke worked her lineback dun alongside Berkley as they walked up the incline. "I've been wondering, Reg, how is it a nice lookin', educated man like yourself isn't married?"

He chuckled. "Almost was…once. I was courting a young lady back in New York until I went off to school at the Colorado School of Mines, nine years ago." Berkley shrugged. "We were going to be engaged...but I recall a line from an anonymous poem in Francis Davison's *Poetical Rhapsody* published in 1602, that is apropos in our case...'Absence makes the heart grow fonder—of somebody else!'...She got married less than a year after I left." He glanced over at her. "I never went back to New York...Stayed out here in the west."

"And been too busy ever since?"

He nodded. "Something like that."

"My mother had me read Shakespeare's *Othello,* he wrote in 1604, that speaks of that when Desdemona confessed, 'I dote upon his very absence.'...Apparently not always true, I suppose."

Silke paused as she reflected on Ranger Riley Boston recuperating from his gunshot induced concussion back in Gainesville. *Wonder if he's goin' to wait for me?*

Berkley glanced at her again. "Romance writers tend to write more with wishful thinking and idealism than reality."

"Always have...and probably always will."

He smiled. "Not altogether a bad thing, I suppose. Gives us commoners something to aspire to."

The sun was a little past its apex as they neared Glorieta Mesa—Thompson Peak was easily visible to the north.

Berkley trotted up to Bone and Loraine at the front. Haven was taking her turn leading Ted with Bear Dog perched on top of the panniers, sitting on his haunches and looking ahead like the captain of a ship.

"Well, according to my directions, this is where I leave you good folks and head south to the Circle W Ranch…Will have to say, it has been interesting."

Bone reached over and shook Berkley's hand. "Oh, I'm sure we'll cross paths again."

He nodded and smiled. "Hopefully sooner than later."

"We'll see."

He touched the brim of his gray Homberg, nodded to the ladies, winked at Elizabeth, reined his blood bay gelding to the left and trotted off south down the valley…

They watched him leave and nudged their mounts into a nice single foot the last five miles to Santa Fe along the winding trail through the canyons.

A little over an hour later, they rode into the south side of Santa Fe on the Pecos Trail.

Silke turned to Elizabeth. "Just so you know, honey, Santa Fe was founded in 1610 by the Governor from Spain, *Pedro de Peralta.* But it had actually been an Indian settlement since about the year 900."

"Really?…That was a long time ago, wasn't it?"

"It was indeed."

Bone pointed to his right. "Thompson Peak is about five miles due east…there."

"And the Santa Fe River ran through here until the 1700s…Since dried up as rivers sometimes do," added Silke.

"Why?"

"They just do…lotsa reasons. Like people an' animals…Had run its time, I guess."

Haven turned in her saddle to look around. "All the buildin's are adobe style, aren't they?"

"And have been for hundreds of years and probably will continue to be so for the foreseeable future," commented Loraine.

Bone looked over at his wife. "At least you speak the lingo, if we need it, babe."

The former Loraine Rodriguez, now Bone, grinned. "You think?"

Bone nodded his head to an adobe building on their right with pole corrals attached on the side. "Funny they got corrals on the side of a library."

Loraine looked over and laughed. "*Librea* is Spanish for Livery not library."

Bone grinned. "Who knew?" He reined over to the front.

The others followed.

"Pard, why don't you trundle in there and ask the proprietor if he knows how to get to the Bar M Ranch."

Loraine grinned as she dismounted. "Good idea Bone. Be a lot faster than you trying to ask in TexMex…Hey comprado, knowee the wayee to the Bar M Ranchito, Signor?" She shook her head as she headed inside the wide front doors.

"Works back home," Bone said to her back.

He led everyone over to the water trough to let the animals catch up on their hydration. Bear Dog jumped down and helped himself.

They were still drinking when Loraine came back out with a Mexican in typical peasant garb and a straw sombrero still chattering at her as they walked over to the others.

She turned when they got to the group and nodded to the hostler. "*Muchas gracias amigo...ten un buen dia en el trabajo*."

He pulled his hat from his head, held it in both hands and bowed slightly and grinning before turning and walking back inside. "*De nada señora, de nada. Vaya con Dios.*"

Loraine stuck her foot into the stirrup on Sweet Face's left side and swung lithely into the saddle. "*Sígueme así chico y chicas...y andele pronto. Nosotros vamos.*" She reined around, pointed, and trotted off back to the south.

Bone frowned as he followed her. "Huh?"

Haven trotted up beside him. "She said, 'follow me this way, boy an' girls, walk quickly. We go'."

"Why didn't she just say that?"

Silke rode up to his other side. "She's your wife…ask her."

Bone shook his head. "Uh-uh…She'll hurt me."

§§§

CHAPTER TWENTY-FIVE

BAR M RANCH

"We'll be back d'rectly…'Fore supper 'spect, Miz Luz. Gonna go check that ridge." Jack Tarbutton looked at the two other Bar M hands, Merkins White, and Pablo Armendáriz. "Let's go, boys."

Luz McPherson watched them ride out with no little trepidation.

The three ranch hands nudged their horses into a lope heading to the north west.

They easy loped their mounts through the main pasture in the center of Bobcat Canyon. The Bar M horse herd was belly deep in good spring grass. They looked up unconcernedly as the three riders passed through to the ridge a mile further north and to the west.

Jake or the other Bar M hands couldn't see the group with Silke, Bone, Haven, Loraine, and Elizabeth headed south toward the headquarters on the east side of the valley. Their eyes were focused on the four horses up at the top of the ridge another three hundred yards away.

The lanky foreman nodded to the other two. "'Bout what I figured."

They bumped their horses up into a medium gallop up the side of the ridge. Jake held up his hand to stop as they broke back down into a lope, then a trot, finally a full stop twenty feet from the four Circle W riders.

"What's goin' on here?" asked Jake.

Ty Needham pitched his half-smoked quirly to the ground, crushed it with the toe of his boot, and looked up at Tarbutton. "That's none of yer business."

"Well, I beg to differ. You boys is on Bar M ground an' that makes it my business."

The three other hands were gathering loose rocks and putting them in a gunny sack.

Needham feigned a surprised look. "Bar M? Why we though we's on Circle W land…ain't that right boys?"

"Shore, Ty, that's what we thought, awright." Eb Marsh chuckled as did the other two.

Jake pushed his hat back from his face with a thumb. "Nice try. The Circle W is over a mile thataway." He pointed to the east across the valley.

Ty laid the palm of his right hand on the stag grip of his Colt. "You callin' me a liar?"

Bone and the group trotted up to the rambling adobe style ranch house and pulled rein out front.

"Hello the house," he shouted.

Loraine leaned over. "Hacienda."

"Hacienda…Hello the hacienda."

Luz McPherson stepped through the screendoor with her '73 Winchester at her hip, pointed at

Bone. "Who are you, big man, an' what do you want?"

Bone pulled his dark green John Bull hat from his head. "Name's Bone, Ma'am." He glanced to his left. "This is my wife, Loraine, that's Silke Justice, her cousin, Haven Justice…that's Bear Dog beside Silke…and that cute little girl next to her…is your granddaughter…Elizabeth Haas."

Luz took a step backward, her eyes big as saucers, and leaned her rifle against the wall next to the door. "Whoo, whoo, oh my. Oh, my…Lordamercy. Whoo!" She ran down the four steps to the ground, over to Elizabeth and Calico. "Get down here, child, let me look at you."

She slid out of the saddle where Luz grabbed both shoulders, looked her full in the face, and then pulled her close in a tight hug. "Oh, my, you look just like yer mama, Sarah."

"Are you my grandma?"

Tears rolled down Luz's cheeks. "Never thought I'd get to hear those words." She looked down at Elizabeth's eyes. "Yes, honey, I'm yer grandma."

She finally looked over at Bone and the ladies. "Why didn't ya'll let me know you were comin'?...An' where's my boys?"

The others exchanged glances.

Silke dismounted. "Think we best go in the house, Ma'am...Need to talk."

"Oh, pshaw, call me Luz...The rest of you git down, git down." She kept her arm wrapped around Elizabeth's shoulder as the others also stepped down from their mounts.

Bone looked at her. "Uh...Luz, mind if we tend to our animals first. They could use some water."

"My men are out checkin' on somethin', so you'll have to take care of them yerselves. Pull yer tack an' put 'em in the corral with my horses...There's a water trough in there an' alfalfa hay's already been put out for the others...I'll git Martina to put on some coffee. She baked some *Polvorones de Canele*."

Bone leaned over to Loraine and looked into her deep brown eyes.

"Cinnamon cookies."

"Oh, yum."

Jake shook his head at the gunslick. "Ain't nobody said nothin' 'bout lyin'...Mebe you jest fergot where the Circle W stopped."

"Sounds to me like yer callin' me a liar...an' I don't tolerate that from no man." Ty slicked his Colt from the well-used holster and fired one shot, hitting Jake in the center of his chest with an audible thump.

The slim foreman threw up his hands and flipped backward from his saddle, dead when he hit the ground. His horse squealed in fright at the shot and shied to the right into Merkins' pony.

The shocked Bar M cowboy managed to gather his reins and settle his horse down. Both he and Pablo were frozen as they stared at the gunman in surprise.

Ty turned to Eb and the others. "He was goin' fer his gun...Ya'll seen it. Self-defense." Needham looked back at the two ranch hands. "Ya'll best load him up on his nag an' leave us be...less'n one of you wants to call me a liar, too."

Merkins just glared at the hired gun as Pablo rounded up Jake's horse.

Luz and Elizabeth were on the porch, almost to the door when they heard a distant gunshot in the still afternoon air.

A look of fear crossed Luz's face. She glanced back at Bone's group as they had most of the tack pulled and the panniers unloaded from Ted. They were looking off to the northwest, too—then at her.

"Trouble?" Bone called out to her.

She pursed her lips. "Hope not." Luz opened the screendoor and ushered Elizabeth inside the cool semi-darkness of the interior.

Silke was first to lead her gelding to the corral gate and turn him inside. He immediately kicked up his heels, jumped around a few times before dropping to his knees, laying on his side and rolling in the dirt—happy to be free from his saddle and knowing his day's work was done.

Haven followed next with *d'Artagnan*, then Loraine with Sweet Face. Bone came behind her, leading Hildebrandt and Ted. They all took their turns in rolling in the dirt.

Silke went back and had Calico's reins and led him inside where she pulled the headstall free and eased the snaffle bit from his mouth.

Bone closed and latched the cedar pole gate after she came back out. They turned and headed to the hacienda where Loraine and Haven waited on the porch.

As Loraine reached to open the door, they heard horses galloping up from the north.

Two men, one of them leading a third horse with a body tied across the saddle, slowed to a walk, then stopped in front of the porch.

Luz came back out the door, followed closely by Elizabeth. "Merkins! Is he…?"

The cowboy nodded. "Yessum, that gunhawk of Wilford, Ty Needham, shot him dead. Shot him right through the heart, he did."

Pablo nodded. "*Señor* Tarbutton…no had chance."

"Needham claimed Jake was goin' fer his gun, but both his hands was crossed on top of his saddlehorn cap all the time they was talkin'…Murdered 'im, plain an' simple…Said he was callin' him a liar."

Luz looked at him. "Was he, Merkins?"

He shook his head. "No, Ma'am. Jake jest told them they were on Bar M land…the gunslinger said they thought they were on Circle W property…They wuz four of 'em an' they all laughed when he said it."

She looked at Bone. "They knew where they were. Circle W is over a mile from that ridge, 'cross the valley…it's nowhere close." She looked back at her employee. "Could ya'll tell what they were doin' up there?"

White shrugged his shoulders. "Jest pickin' up rocks an' puttin' 'em in a toesack…Made no sense atall."

"What kind of rocks are up there, Miz McPherson?" asked Silke.

She shook her head. "I don't know. Never been up there…Ground's no good fer nothin' 'cept'n mebe sheep."

"What color of rocks were they picking up?" asked Bone.

For the first time, Merkins White noticed the big man. He looked back at Luz.

"They're from Texas. That's Mister Bone. They brought my granddaughter to me."

Bone pulled out a deputy marshal's badge from his pocket. "We're authorized law officers, Luz, my wife and I…Silke is a Pinkerton detective." He glanced back at the ranch hand. "Could you tell what they were picking up?"

He shrugged his shoulders again. "Jest some white, kinda shiny lookin' rocks…best could tell."

Bone glanced at Loraine and Silke. "White quartz…good source for finding silver or gold."

Silke nodded. "Circle W…That's where he said he was headed." She looked at Luz. "We had a man travelin' with us from Texas who was a minin' engineer…had some work to do for the owner of the Circle W." She looked at White. "Was there a city slicker type with them?"

Merkins shook his head. "No, Miss…They were all Circle W cowhands…Knowed ever one of 'em."

"They probably didn't have time to know he was headed to their ranch, not to say anything about gettin' there," offered Haven.

Silke nodded. "True."

"Cain't do nothin' 'bout that now." Luz looked at her cowboys. "Unload Jake over to the bunkhouse. I'll send Martina out to wrap 'im up…God bless his sweet soul…an' git him ready. We'll bury him out by the orchard tomorra…Pablo, want to go into Santa Fe in the mornin' an' tell Sheriff Russell."

"*Si, Señora.*"

The men turned their lathered horses and walked them toward the bunkhouse near the barn taking Jake's body with them.

Luz led everyone inside to the main large room off the kitchen. There was a low fire in the five feet wide, four feet high stone fireplace. The room was nice and toasty.

"Ya'll have a seat. I'll have Martina bring out some coffee." She looked down at Elizabeth. "Would you like some lemonade, sweet thing?"

"Yes, Ma'am, thank you."

Luz looked at the others and winked. "My daughter did a good job." She walked into the kitchen.

The full-figured Mexican cook, Martina, came right out with a metal tray and five cups of coffee. She set it on a large round low table between the two hair out cowhide couches from multicolored longhorns, studded up and down the front arms and across the bottom with large dome-topped brass tacks.

Luz followed behind her with a large tumbler of fresh lemonade that she set down in front of Elizabeth sitting cross-legged on the floor in front of the fireplace with Bear Dog.

She picked up one of the earthenware cups and sat down in a matching, overstuffed chair across from the couches and leaned forward—her elbows on her knees. “Now, where are my boys?”

§§§

CHAPTER TWENTY-SIX

CIRCLE W RANCH

Ty Needham and the three other hands walked across the flagstone to the ornate carved front door of Ben Wilford's adobe hacienda. The thick door had a small glassed rectangle at eye height and was hung to the jamb by thick, two inch wide, hammered iron strap hinges that extended over two-thirds across the face. Pak Cole carried the partially filled burlap sack.

Wilford and Berkley sat in the large open front room, each with a snifter of brandy.

Ben looked up. "How'd it go?"

Needham's lip curled up in a lopsided sneer. "Got yer samples. Foreman an' two others rode up whilst we were collectin' 'em." His sneer expanded in a self-congratulatory full grin. "That old lady is short one foreman."

Wilford shot to his feet. "What? You shot him?"

His sneer returned. "Called me a liar…Didn't he boys?"

Marsh, Cole, and Higgins matched his sneer.

"He did…in so many words," said Marsh with a chuckle.

The other two grinned and nodded.

"Fool!…Damn gun happy fool! Now we're gonna have Sheriff Russell to deal with."

Needham glanced at the others. "Everbody's willin' to swear he drawed first…Right boys?"

The three minions nodded.

"That makes it their word 'gainst ours…two to four. Fair hand to hold, I'd say."

Wilford blew out his breath. "They know what ya'll were pickin' up?"

The gunhawk shook his head. "Didn't appear to…Hell, we didn't know what we were pickin' up. Jest follerin' yer directions." He nodded to Cole who set the dusty bag on the coffee table between the two men. "Who's this?"

"If it's any of your concern, this is Reginald Berkley, a mining engineer I brought in."

Needham shook his head. "Reginald?…Huh."

Berkley glared at him a moment, set his snifter down, opened the bag and dumped the rocks on the table top.

"That's a handmade mahogany table."

Reg's blue eyes snapped to him, and then to the table top. He pulled a small magnifying glass from his pocket, picked up one of the white quartz chunks and studied it with the glass.

Berkley set it down, picked up another one and turned it over in his hand to study all sides. He repeated the procedure with another, larger piece.

Wilford's brown eyes focused on Berkley. "Well?"

He picked up one more, gave it an examination, nodded and looked at the owner of the Circle W.

"Definitely gold veins in the quartz…These samples should grade out high."

"How much is there?"

"That, my good man, is the fly in the buttermilk. There's no way of telling how deep it runs without excavation and further study…May just be an anomaly or the whole damn ridge could be infused…I'd certainly suggest buying the property."

Wilford sat back in his burgundy leather wingback chair and took a of sip of his Napoleon brandy. "That, my dear Berkley is, as you say, another fly in the buttermilk…the witch that owns the property isn't willin' to sell. Been tryin'…Rejected ever offer I've made an' hasn't flinched at other, uh…methods we've tried."

Needham stepped closer. "She ain't got but two hands left, Boss…an' she 'pears a mite peaked."

Wilford nodded. "Think she's got the consumption."

Berkley looked at him. "Wait her out."

Wilford thrust his lower jaw forward. "Waitin' goes 'gainst my nature…Ain't built fer it." He looked at Needham. "Get all the boys together in the mornin' at daylight…We'll go pay the old hag a neighborly visit."

"All of 'em?"

Wilford stared at the gunslinger…

BAR M RANCH

Luz bit her lower lip as the tears silently rolled down her cheeks. Elizabeth got to her feet, sat down beside her grandmother and wrapped both arms around her in support.

She took a deep breath and placed her left arm about the young girl and kissed the top of her blonde head. "Gone…All my babies gone." Luz choked back a sob. "But, I got Lizbeth, now." She looked up. "Thank you, Jesus."

"Grandma, I brought you something."

"What's that, dear child?"

Elizabeth reached into the slash pocket of her dress and pulled out a small velvet box and handed it to her.

Luz looked at her questioningly, and then opened it. "Oh, my…This is exquisitely beautiful, Lizbeth. Where'd you get this?" She held the wine pearl mounted in a gold setting up to the light by its gold chain.

"From Unka James' daughter, my cousin, Maggie."

"And my other granddaughter…but I thought she passed away two years ago?"

Elizabeth nodded. "She did."

"Then how…"

Bone cleared his throat. "Hate to interrupt, Miz Luz, but it's my opinion we have a tenuous situation here and need to make plans."

She looked at him. "I don't understand."

"If that white quartz has in it what I think it does…your neighbor will be looking at it right now. Gold does strange things to people. If he wanted your ranch before…well, just compound that tenfold…How many men do you think they have?"

Luz looked at Elizabeth, then at Bone. "Jake said he had at least ten…an' half are gunhawks."

"Like the one that gunned him down?"

She nodded.

"You've got two hired hands, right?"

"An' neither is a gunhand…they're horse wranglers, not fighters…plus Pablo is headin' to town in the mornin' to get the sheriff."

Bone pursed his lips. "Two hours in…two hours back." He looked at her. "Not going to be soon enough."

"What do you suggest?"

Bone looked at Loraine, Silke, and Haven and grinned. "This is what we do, Luz…Like our motto in the Marine Corps…*Improvidus, Apto, Quod Victum*."

Luz wrinkled her brow.

Silke smiled. "Latin for Improvise, Adapt, and Overcome."

The morning broke with a low dreary overcast at the near seven thousand feet altitude. A heavy, cold, misty fog hugged the ground as Pablo mounted his mustang and trotted north toward Santa Fe.

The kitchen was warm with the heat given off by the wood cook stove. Martina walked around the table with a large blue merle graniteware pot, refilling everyone's cup.

Bone looked over at Merkins White, Luz's remaining wrangler. "Need you to post yourself where you think the Circle W boys would be coming from. Should be able to hear ten men or so on horseback long before they get to you…even in the fog. You get back here and let us know, hear?"

Merkins nodded. "They gotta come through the pass on the east side to git here from the Circle W…Hear 'em comin' down the hill."

"Then you station yourself inside the loft above the barn after you let us know…Got a Winchester?"

"Henry."

"Any good with it?"

"Hit what I aim at."

"Good enough…Stay outta sight."

Merkins nodded, took one last sip of his coffee, got to his feet, and headed to the front door.

Bone looked at Loraine. "Babe, when we get the word from Merkins they're comin', we'll go out the back and take cover on each side of the front of the hacienda…Silke, you and Haven will go out with Luz when they ride up…"

"What if they come in shootin'?"

Bone grinned. "That question doesn't need an answer, does it?"

She smiled. "Not really."

"You and Haven get on each side of Luz and spread apart when she goes out on the porch to see what they want, as she normally would...Right, Luz?"

"With my Winchester at my hip."

"Like when we rode up." Bone grinned.

"Be sure Lizbeth knows to stay back in her bedroom. These adobe walls are way too thick for any type of round to go through." Silke looked at Luz.

"I know...I'll get her prepared when she wakes up."

Bone laid his 500 on the table. "Every one double check your firearms and make sure you have plenty ammo."

Merkins pulled his mount to a stop near a ponderosa pine at the base of the incline to the east, a little south of the notch in the hogback. He kept his eyes and ears focused on what he knew was the pass to the Circle W.

His vision was limited to less than a hundred feet because of the fog—Merkins didn't have long to wait.

The sound of multiple shod horses working their way down the side of the mountain, the steel of their shoes clicked on the rocks.

Merkins spun his horse and galloped the half-mile back to the Bar M headquarters. He reined the cowpony to a sliding stop, his hind feet drew a long set of 11s in the fog damp dirt in front of the barn.

The wrangler dismounted before the horse had finished his slide and sprinted to the house. "They're comin', they're comin'."

Bone burst out the front screendoor. "Any idea how many?"

He shook his head. "A bunch."

"Get to your station." Bone ducked back inside.

Merkins ran back to his horse standing patiently, his reins hanging down, ground tied. He grabbed them, led the animal inside the barn and closed the big double doors behind them.

In a couple of moments, he'd pulled the tack from the horse, put him in a stall and latched the door. Merkins removed his Henry lever-action repeater from his saddle boot and climbed the ladder to the loft. He worked his way to the hay door and cracked it enough to see the house.

Bone and Loraine ducked out the back of the house, Bear Dog stuck with Loraine. Luz, Silke, and Haven gathered at the front door as they could plainly hear the thundering hoof beats of the Circle W riders as they galloped into the yard in front of Luz's hacienda.

Wilford nudged his lathered horse to the front of the gang as they stopped. "Hello the house."

The other eleven riders spread out to his right and left. Berkley eased up beside him as Luz and the girls came out the front door.

She held the Winchester in both hands at her right hip. Silke and Haven moved five feet to either side of her—both had slipped an extra gun in their belt, giving them two.

"What do you want, Wilford?…See you brought a lot of help with you."

Berkley's eyes widened and his jaw dropped as he saw Silke and Haven—even more when he looked at Luz…

§§§

CHAPTER TWENTY-SEVEN

BAR M RANCH

Berkley leaned to Wilford. “Why didn’t you tell me that the owner of this ranch was Luz McPherson?”

He glanced at Berkley. “What the hell for? Just an old woman.”

“I’ve known that ‘old woman’ since I was twelve.” He looked up at Silke and Haven, then around for Bear Dog and Bone and Loraine. "You don't want to do this…You don't have near enough men…trust me on that. I'm done…Don't want any part of this."

Bone and Loraine stepped around their respective corners of Luz's hacienda. He held his .50 caliber pointed at Wilford and Loraine her .45 semiautomatic at him, also.

Wilford noticed Bone and Loraine joining the party and laughed. "The five of you gonna take all of us?"

Silke thumbed the hammer back on her Smith and Wesson 500. "You may get some of us, but you'll never know about it, 'cause you'll be the first to die…This is a .50 caliber handgun an' it's goin' to blow you in two."

Berkley stepped down from his gelding and walked toward Luz's porch.

"Damn you, nobody walks out on me." Wilford drew his Remington and shot Berkley in the back.

Reg staggered two steps and collapsed at the edge of Luz's porch.

The very air erupted in what seemed like a single earsplitting roar as Bone, Silke, Haven, Luz, and Loraine simultaneously fired.

Silke and Bone's three hundred and fifty grain .50 caliber bullets hit Wilford's chest less than an inch apart virtually at the same time and literally blew the rancher's body in two parts, spraying blood on the men on both sides of him.

Loraine triple-tapped his head as it was falling, turning it into a large cloud of red and gray mist like an exploding watermelon before the pieces hit the ground.

Horses screamed and squealed in fear as they danced around in the melee. The Circle W riders were trying to get their guns in play from the backs of the panicked animals.

Bone and Loraine picked new targets as fast as they could pull the triggers.

He emptied his five round cylinder, added five more with his speed loader and continued.

Loraine fired all eight of her bullets, dumped her magazine, slammed another home, thumbed her slide closed and also continued—all in less than three seconds.

Silke calmly stood like an old time duelist and squeezed off round after round. She pulled her spare gun from her belt, a Colt .38-40, and commenced firing with her left hand.

Haven targeted Ty Needham first, drilling the center of the gunhawk's chest and blowing him out of his saddle, then she fanned her Colt, sweeping to her left as she did.

Luz levered her Winchester, loading the .44-40 rounds as fast as was humanly possible—the rifle never left her hip.

Wild, ineffective shots were being fired by the gunslingers from the backs of their bucking and dancing mounts.

Bear Dog sprinted from Loraine's side to the line of raiders and launched his one hundred pounds of muscled fury in a black blur at the nearest man to the far right. He latched onto the gunhawk's throat as he took him from his saddle to the ground.

Two of the hired guns decided they didn't want any more of it, spun their horses about and spurred them viciously toward the entrance.

Silke dropped her empty .50 cal, drew her tomahawk and in one smooth motion threw it at one of the men trying to escape. The razor-edged war hatchet buried itself in the back of the man's head, causing him to pitch forward over his mount's head to the ground where the horse trampled him as it ran on. It didn't matter because he was dead before he left his saddle.

The last rider panic spurred his horse past the barn as he tried to get away from the slaughter. A shot rang out from the loft and the man pitched from his saddle and tumbled across the ground several times before coming to a stop against the base of a cottonwood tree like a rag doll.

Merkins peeked out from the open loft door to admire his handy work.

Silence abruptly descended on the Bar M headquarters. A huge cloud of gunsmoke, mixed with the morning fog, hung like some malignant growth over the area.

Luz looked around at the carnage of twelve dead men, and two horses that had caught wild shots, in mute evidence of the violence just ended.

There were pockmarks in the adobe wall of her ranch house behind her, plus gouges in the pine plank floor of her porch around her feet.

Bone stepped forward from the corner of the hacienda. "Everybody all right?" He looked over at Loraine as she slipped a fresh magazine in her .45 out of habit and racked the slide. "Babe?"

"I'm good, Bone." She put her very warm Kimber back in its holster.

Silke picked up her 500 where she had dropped it when she pulled her tomahawk. "Gotta get me some of those speed loadin' things for my .50, Bone."

"Think you're out of luck till Padrino can make a trip, Silke."

She looked over at Haven. "All right, cuz?"

The raven-haired young beauty nodded. "Think I'm goin' to start wearin' a double rig."

Bear Dog padded up on the porch to be beside Silke, blood still dripped from his muzzle as he dropped to his haunches, grinning and looking around as if to say, 'Are we done?'.

A moan came from the bottom of the steps.

Haven jumped down from the porch and knelt beside Berkley. "Reg, oh, I was so scared he'd killed you." She gently rolled him to his back and laid his head in her lap.

His eyes fluttered. "You mean I'm not dead?"

Haven wiped a tear from her eye. "No, not yet." She looked up at Bone. "We need to get him inside, an' stop this bleeding."

Bone grinned. "Say no more." He stepped down from the porch, bent over, cradled the one hundred and eighty pound Berkley like a child, and carried him through the screendoor being held open by Luz.

"Bring him this way, Bone."

She led them down the hallway, catching a glimpse of Elizabeth's back as she scurried into her room. Luz stopped at her open doorway. "I'll deal with you later, young lady." She turned to her right and opened the door to a spare bedroom in the spacious hacienda.

She pointed to a patchwork quilt on a brass double bed. "Put him there and let's get those bloody clothes off…I'll get Martina from her hiding place in the pantry to get some water on to boil an' bring back some towels."

Loraine and Haven assisted in getting the bloody clothing off Berkley as Bone held him up. He drifted in and out of consciousness as they finally got his under shirt over his head.

Bone examined the wound. "Through and through…Don't see any bubbles. I'd say he was lucky."

Loraine shook her head. "If you can say getting shot is lucky."

Luz came back in with a stack of towels and a clean sheet to rip into strips for bandages.

"Babe, get my medical kit out of my saddlebags, think we dropped them in the big room in the corner…Luz, do you have any whiskey or tequila handy?"

"Be right back."

Loraine hurried out of the room behind Luz and in less than half a minute came back in with his black leather med kit.

Luz came in on her heels with a bottle of Sauza tequila. She was followed by Martina with a pan of hot water since she already had a tea kettle on the stove.

Bone had checked the wound for cloth and any other debris while they were gone.

He pulled the cork from the bottle with his teeth and spat it to the floor. "Luz, hold that hole open wide as you can."

She put her hands on both sides of the wound, pressed and pulled, opening it wider while Bone poured some of the strong alcohol directly into the hole after placing a folded towel under his back, covering the entrance wound.

"Glad he's unconscious." He lifted him up enough to check the blood tinged tequila running out of his back between his spine and shoulder blade.

Loraine wiped the excess blood from his front with a cloth she had dipped in the hot water while Bone opened the kit and took a vial of white powder out, sprinkled some on the quarter-sized exit wound on the right of his upper chest. He lifted him up and handed the vial to Loraine to do the same on the dime-sized entrance wound after cleaning most of the blood off with another damp cloth.

The flow of blood quickly stopped.

"What is that?" asked Luz.

Bone shrugged. "Powdered alum. Learned about it from Deputy US Marshal Selden Lindsey on a case we were working with Bass Reeves up in the Nations a while back…Works great."

"I see."

"He got it from his barber who used an alum stick for razor nicks."

Bone's strong hands tore a clean white towel in four pieces, folded one into a pad as Loraine folded another. They pressed them over the wounds already showing massive bruising from the impact of the .45 caliber bullet.

Luz ripped one of her clean sheets into four inch wide strips and handed them to Loraine as she did.

Bone held Berkley upright as Loraine wrapped the strips around his chest and over his right shoulder, securing the pads in place.

"We'll have to change this in the morning," said Loraine.

"Is he going to be all right?"

They turned to see Elizabeth standing in the doorway, her hands were clasped together in front of her chest. There was a look of concern on her face.

Bone smiled. "I think so, Lizbeth…long as infection doesn't set in…He's going to need a lot of care."

She pursed her little rosebud lips. "I'll help."

Luz knelt down in front of her and pulled her into a hug. "Thank you, honey, I know he'll appreciate that."

"Luz, heard him say he'd known you since he was twelve…What's that about?"

She rose to her feet and kept one arm about Elizabeth's shoulder.

Luz looked at Reg for a long moment before she turned to Silke. "It's a bit of a story."

§§§

EPILOGUE

BAR M RANCH

"I would rather wait till Reginald is awake before I tell the story…I think he's going to want to hear it, too."

They were in the big main room, sitting around and having some much needed coffee when the sound of thundering hooves pierced the thick adobe walls from outside and interrupted Luz.

She looked up from one of the couches. "Looks like Sheriff Russell made good time." Luz got to her feet.

The others followed suit and moved with her to the door. She went out first, the rest followed.

The tall, trim, gray-haired lawman sat his horse in front of the fifteen man posse from Santa Fe—he rested both hands on top of his saddlehorn.

Pablo was beside him on his lathered sorrel gelding.

Sheriff Russell glanced around at all the bodies. "Dang, Luz, looks like ya'll had a bit of a war out here. Sorry we missed the party…told you he wuz gonna be upset."

"Well, that's not really it, Case…Why don't you an' yer boys step down, water those poor horses an' let 'em blow a bit…then come in the house. I'll see that Martina has 'nough coffee. Think she baked some cookies, too…Fill you in."

"*Señora*, I go rub down my *caballo* an' feed heem. He work hard."

"Go ahead Pablo, you can go in the kitchen when you finish. Martina will fix you a good lunch."

"*Si, Señora, muchas gracias*."

Thirty minutes later, Luz finished telling the sheriff the events of the morning as well as about Jake Tarbutton's murder yesterday afternoon.

Sheriff Case Russell grinned and shook his head. "Gosh dang, Luz, the five of you took care of all those miscreants?…Don't that blow yer hat over the windmill." He wiped his forehead with his kerchief. "Know of some of those boys out there on the ground…mean as a skillet full of rattlers."

She smiled. "Silke's wolf dog there…" Luz pointed at Bear Dog asleep in front of the fireplace. "…participated an' took out one of 'em."

"You don't say?…'Peers as they let their bulldog mouths overload their jaybird asses, ask me." The sheriff took a sip of his coffee. "Send a couple wagons out from town to haul the bodies back to the undertaker…Jest gotta figure out how the county is gonna pay fer plantin' all of 'em."

"We haven't looked, Sheriff, but I'll bet a dollar to a donut you'll find enough in that Wilford's pockets…Strikes me as the type to carry a wad of cash on him."

Case looked over at Bone. "Could be right, Deputy Bone, could be right." He changed his focus back to Luz. "Be sendin' the doc out to take a gander of that young engineer feller what got shot, too."

"Be much obliged, Case…Now, 'nybody needin' more coffee?"

The sheriff rose to his feet and grabbed his hat from the big low table in the center of the room where he'd laid it. "We best git headed back to town, Luz. Need to get the undertaker out here with his wagons for the bodies 'fore they turn ripe…"

He paused at the door. "Don't see no problem you keepin' all the guns, tack an' them boy's mounts…fer all the trouble they caused ya'll."

Luz grinned. "May take us a while to round 'em all up. Scattered like a covey of quail when the shootin' started an' they lost their riders…I'm a bit shorthanded since they killed poor Jake."

Deputy Shorty Henry glanced at the sheriff. "Uh…Sheriff, you don't mind, I'd like to ask Miz Luz if'n she'd like me to work for her…Really enjoy workin' with horses."

"Up to you, Shorty."

Luz nodded. "You're hired, Shorty…You were always a good worker. Bring your gear an' put it in the bunkhouse…Can you start right away helpin' us round up that stock?"

He looked to the sheriff who just smiled and nodded.

"Yessum."

Two hours later, the sun was settling behind the mountains to the west. Everyone sat around the big room with after dinner coffee.

Silke turned to Haven. "Well, cuz, I'd have to say you've passed your tests to become a Pinkerton."

"I what?"

"You don't think I haven't been watchin'?"

She set her cup on the small table to the side of her chair. "Uh…I really didn't know."

"The only thing is we'll have to catch the train to Denver to the regional office to get you sworn in…assumin' you still want to be a detective."

Haven shot to her feet. "Yes, yes, of course." Her white, even teeth gleamed as a smile spread across her face.

Loraine turned to Silke. "There's a train from Santa Fe to Denver?"

"Yes, has been for a while."

Loraine glanced at Bone. "Did you know there was a train from Denver to Santa Fe?"

He had a sheepish grin on his face. "Uh, yeah, babe."

"And there's the Gulf and Colorado that goes through Gainesville to Denver?"

"Uh-huh…that too."

Loraine's brow furrowed. "So, we could have taken the train from Gainesville to Denver, and then Denver down to Santa Fe and not have to make that God-awful trek across the *Llano*?"

"Uh…well…yeah."

"Damn you, Bone…I'm going to hurt you."

He held up both hands. "Sorry, babe, I'd just never seen the Palo Duro Canyon and thought this would be a good chance."

Loraine wagged her finger at him and opened her mouth to read him the riot act, but was interrupted by Elizabeth as she came in the room. She had been sitting with Reginald Berkley.

"Mister Berkley is awake an' wants a glass of water."

Luz got to her feet. "Well, we'll just have to take care of that." She looked around the room at the others. "Looks like a good time for a story."

"Martina!" she yelled to her cook through the other doorway to the kitchen. "Please bring some cool water for Mister Berkley."

"*Sí, señora.*"

Luz headed to the hallway followed by the others to Reg's room and walked in.

"How are you feelin'?"

He blinked a couple of times and grimaced. "Like I've been shot."

Martina came in just after the others with the water and handed it to Luz.

She cupped the back of his head, lifted it up and held the tumbler to his dry lips. "Easy now, you sure don't wanta choke."

Reg blinked in agreement as he slowly drained the glass.

"More?"

He shook his head. "Not right now."

"We probably should prop him up a bit so he doesn't get pneumonia," suggested Bone.

Luz grabbed a couple of pillows from the cedar chest while Bone raised his upper body and she stuffed them behind him. "There, how's that?"

He nodded. "Better."

Luz sat down on the side of the bed at his feet. "Reg, I promised these folks I would fill them in about our history together…an' there's some things you aren't aware of."

He held up his left hand a little. "I have a confession to make first."

Luz frowned. "A confession?"

He bit his lip against the pain. "I originally started out on the trip out here to steal the three…three pounds of pearls I thought they carried…and I hired some men to rob them on the trail, but weren't to hurt anyone."

"Don't think they got the memo," commented Bone.

Reg groaned. "Apparently…But as I grew to know everybody, especially Elizabeth…couldn't go through with it."

"But you couldn't pull those toughs off then."

He looked at Silke and shook his head. "Uh-uh…As it…as it turned out, you, Bone, Loraine, and…and Haven proved to be more than a match for them…I've never been more relieved…Just had to get it off my chest. Can't say how sorry I am."

Silke reached forward and took his hand. "That was you in the jewelry store wasn't it?"

He nodded.

"God works in mysterious ways his wonders to perform…as the hymn goes."

He looked up at Silke and nodded again.

"We have a saying back home…No harm, no foul," said Bone.

Luz pulled Elizabeth to sit down beside her. "Now, for my story…Reg's family an' mine were neighbors back east in White Plains, New York. My twins, Timothy an' James were seven years older than my Sarah, Elizabeth's mama, an' Reginald…an' they got wild hairs an' traipsed off to join the British army to see the world…"

"That's when they fought in the Boer War?" asked Loraine.

Luz nodded. "Well, as young people living close together will do, Reginald an' Sarah started courtin' when they were both eighteen."

Elizabeth looked at Luz, then at Berkley.

"It went on for a while an' they discussed gettin' engaged, but Reg said he should get his education out of the way so he could support them proper an' he left for the west and the Colorado School of Mines…Sarah was devastated and angry."

"I'm so sorry, Luz."

"Wasn't your fault, I thought it was admirable that you wanted to be able to support your family…but Sarah didn't think so an' started seeing a bit older man who already had a job with the railroad…Less than six weeks after you left, she married Charlie Haas."

A look of sadness came over Reg's face as he pressed his lips together.

"A few months after they were married, she told me she was pregnant an' seven months later…Elizabeth was born."

Luz looked at Reg for a long moment, then at the others, and finally to Elizabeth. "What no one but Sarah and me knew was…she was pregnant when she and Charlie married…but it wasn't his."

Silke and Haven exchanged glances as did Bone and Loraine.

Luz took a breath and wrapped her arm around Elizabeth. “Sarah didn’t want to ruin Reg’s chance at an education, so she married Charlie Haas...He never knew.” She looked at Reg. “She refused to let you know...that Elizabeth is your daughter.”

Elizabeth sucked her breath in and looked up at Luz. “Mister Berkley is my real daddy, grandma?”

Luz nodded. “Yes, honey...he’s your real daddy.”

Everyone’s eyes in the room filled. Silke and Haven hugged—Bone put his arm around Loraine and pulled her close.

Huge tears rolled down Elizabeth’s cheeks as she brought her hand to her mouth. Her lower lip quivered and she started breathing rapidly. “I got a daddy...I got a daddy.”

She leaned over and wrapped her arms carefully around Reg as tears poured down his stubbled cheeks, too. “I got a daddy.”

He held her close with his left arm. “Yes, baby, you have a daddy...I love you.”

§§§§§

PREVIEW
the Next Exciting Novel

from

TIMBER CREEK PRESS

ANGEL JUSTICE

CHAPTER ONE

SANTA FE COUNTY

A bullet cracked past Silke's head and buried itself in the bed behind her and Bear Dog as she drove Luz's buckboard toward town to get supplies. The boom of a long gun sounded a little over a half second later. The black, blue-eyed wolf dog turned and looked where the bullet hit and cocked his head.

Silke was on the right side, Luz sat in the middle, and Haven on the left.

Haven pointed at a ball of white smoke around two hundred yards up the side of the mountain in a copse of pinion pine. “There!”

“Hyaa! Hyaa!”

Silke popped the reins over the rumps of the matched set of sorrel geldings pulling the wagon. Dust boiled up behind them as the two well-trained horses reached their top speed.

Luz levered off three quick shots at the smoke with her ’73 Winchester. There was no return fire.

Silke eased back on the ribbons as they rounded a curve and were hidden from the grove of trees where the shot came from.

Silke and Haven Justice were first cousins and virtual look-alikes including their cerulean blue eyes. The major exception—Silke’s long hair was strawberry blonde and Haven’s was raven with a few red highlights. Silke was three years older than the eighteen year old Haven.

Both had their hair in a single long thick braid. Oddly, Silke's naturally draped over her left shoulder and Haven's, her right.

Silke trotted the pair of geldings into the large downtown Santa Fe market square. There were numerous kiosks of local farmers with their produce and Amerindian tribes of Pueblo, Navajo, and Jicarilla Apache selling blankets, pottery, and handmade silver and turquoise jewelry.

Luz McPherson was the sixty year old owner of the horse ranch where the girls were staying. They, along with Bone and Loraine, had brought Luz's granddaughter, nine year old Elizabeth, out from Texas to her.

A fifth member of the group on the trek out was Reginald Berkley, a mining engineer, who, unbeknownst to either himself or Elizabeth at the time—was actually her biological father.

He had been recently wounded by a neighboring rancher when the rancher's gang attacked Luz's ranch in an effort to run her off because of a gold deposit he had discovered on her property. Berkley was currently recovering at her ranch, the Bar M with his new found daughter watching over him.

Luz turned to Silke. "Best we go by Sheriff Russell's office an' report bein' shot at."

"Which way?"

"Turn right up there." She pointed. "His office is only a block that way."

Silke pulled the team to a stop in front of the sheriff's office, a standard thick-walled adobe building for Santa Fe, except the sparse windows were barred with steel rods.

They stepped down, Haven unhooked the lead line from the horse's harness and tied the team to a peeled cedar rail in front of the office. Bear Dog jumped out of the bed to join the ladies as they entered the door.

The trim gray-haired lawman looked up from the paperwork on his cluttered desk. The front room of the combination office and jail smelled of the hot coffee on the pot bellied stove in the corner.

"Well, what do I owe the pleasure, ladies?" He got to his feet out of respect.

Luz put her hands on her narrow hips. "Somebody took a shot at us 'bout a mile out of town, Case. Around two hundred yards up the side of the mountain from some pinion pines."

"Nobody hit?"

Silke shook her head. "You can come look at the hole in the back of the buckboard. Didn't sound like a .44-40, more like a .45-70."

"Almost have to be for that distance." The sheriff nodded. "I'll go out in a bit an' see as I can find anythin'…know that copse of pinions. Just need to finish what I'm workin' on."

"Something serious?" asked Haven.

"Could say…Got a rash of teenage Indian girls been disappearin'…without a trace."

Silke and Haven exchanged glances.

"Pinkertons were called in to solve a case like this last year up in the Nations," said Silke.

"What was it?"

Silke looked him in the eye, pressed her lips together, then took a breath. "You've heard of the Yellow Slave Trade of course…this was Brown Slave Trade."

§§

OTHER NOVELS FROM
TIMBER CREEK PRESS
www.timbercreekpress.net

MILITARY ACTION/TECHNO

BLACK EAGLE FORCE: Eye of the Storm (Book #1)
by Buck Stienke and Ken Farmer

BLACK EAGLE FORCE: Sacred Mountain (Book #2) by Buck Stienke and Ken Farmer

RETURN of the STARFIGHTER (Book #3)
by Buck Stienke and Ken Farmer

BLACK EAGLE FORCE: BLOOD IVORY (Book #4)
by Buck Stienke and Ken Farmer with Doran Ingrham

BLACK EAGLE FORCE: FOURTH REICH (Book #5) by Buck Stienke and Ken Farmer

AURORA: INVASION (Book #6 in the BEF) by Ken Farmer & Buck Stienke

BLACK EAGLE FORCE: ISIS (Book #7) by Buck Stienke and Ken Farmer

BLOOD BROTHERS - Doran Ingrham, Buck Stienke and Ken Farmer

DARK SECRET - Doran Ingrham

NICARAGUAN HELL - Doran Ingrham

BLACKSTAR BOMBER by T.C. Miller

BLACKSTAR BAY by T.C. Miller

BLACKSTAR MOUNTAIN by T.C. Miller
BLACKSTAR ENIGMA by T.C. Miller

HISTORICAL FICTION WESTERN
THE NATIONS by Ken Farmer and Buck Stienke
HAUNTED FALLS by Ken Farmer and Buck Stienke
HELL HOLE by Ken Farmer
ACROSS the RED by Ken Farmer and Buck Stienke
BASS and the LADY by Ken Farmer and Buck Stienke
DEVIL'S CANYON by Buck Stienke
LADY LAW by Ken Farmer
BLUE WATER WOMAN by Ken Farmer
FLYNN by Ken Farmer
AURALI RED by Ken Farmer
COLDIRON by Ken Farmer
STEELDUST by Ken Farmer
BONE by Ken Farmer
BONE'S LAW by Ken Farmer
BONE & LORAINE by Ken Farmer
BONE'S GOLD by Ken Farmer
BONE'S ENIGMA by Ken Farmer
SILKE JUSTICE by Ken Farmer
SILKE'S QUEST by Ken Farmer

NO TIME to DIE by Buck Stienke
SILKE'S RIDE by Ken Farmer

SY/FY
LEGEND of AURORA by Ken Farmer & Buck Stienke
AURORA: INVASION (Book #6 in the BEF) by Ken Farmer & Buck Stienke

HISTORICAL FICTION ROMANCE
THE TEMPLAR TRILOGY
MYSTERIOUS TEMPLAR by Adriana Girolami
THE CRIMSON AMULET by Adriana Girolami
TEMPLAR'S REDEMPTION by Adriana Girolami

MYSTERY
BONE'S PARADOX by Buck Stienke
RECIPE for MURDER by Ken Farmer & Buck Stienke
SIN NO MORE by Ken Farmer & Buck Stienke

Coming Soon

HISTORICAL FICTION WESTERN
McGRATH by T.C. Miller
ANGEL JUSTICE by Ken Farmer

HISTORICAL FICTION ROMANCE
DAUGHTER of HADES by Adriana Girolami
ZAMINDAR and the LADY by Adriana Girolami

SY/FY
ANTAREAN DILEMMA by T.C. Miller

MYSTERY
NIGHT KILL by Ken Farmer & Buck Stienke

Thanks for reading *SILKE'S RIDE* If you enjoyed it, I would really appreciate a review on Amazon. My Author Page is:
www.amazon.com/Ken-Farmer/e/B0057OT3YI
SILKE'S RIDE -
www.amazon.com/dp/B084D1JG1B
Email - pagact@yahoo.com

Personally autographed books available at our web site:
Web page: www.TimberCreekPress.net

TIMBER CREEK PRESS

www.ingramcontent.com/pod-product-compliance
Lightning Source LLC
Chambersburg PA
CBHW022028260626
47156CB00017B/469
* 9 7 8 1 7 3 4 1 7 6 5 3 7 *